I0609337

Florence Henniker

**Foiled**

Vol. III

Florence Henniker

**Foiled**
*Vol. III*

ISBN/EAN: 9783744788908

Printed in Europe, USA, Canada, Australia, Japan

Cover: Foto ©Andreas Hilbeck / pixelio.de

More available books at **www.hansebooks.com**

# FOILED

## VOL. III.

# FOILED

BY

## THE HON. MRS. HENNIKER

AUTHOR OF

"SIR GEORGE," ETC.

"Where sorrow treads on joy,
  Where sweet things soonest cloy,
Where faiths are built on dust,
Where love is half mistrust."

IN THREE VOLUMES

VOL. III.

LONDON:

HURST AND BLACKETT, LIMITED,

13, GREAT MARLBOROUGH STREET.

1893.

*All Rights Reserved.*

RICHARD CLAY & SONS, LIMITED,
LONDON & BUNGAY.

# CONTENTS OF VOLUME III.

## PART III.—(*Continued.*)

# PART III.—(*Continued.*)

# FOILED.

## CHAPTER VI.

### A HIGHLAND PICNIC, AND ITS CONSEQUENCES.

" THIS is an ideal day for a picnic ! The early rain has made everything smell so fresh and sweet, and now the sun is becoming powerful. No, thank you, Frank, I'll start on foot ; Mrs. Gore and Mrs. Forester can ride, and I'll walk with you."

Léo's face looked very bright, and her blue eyes shone with almost childish anticipation as she spoke. By twelve o'clock the party were under weigh, Mrs. Gore leading the procession with the adoring Anthony

alongside, Lords Huddersfield and Strathmashie and one or two other men walking
abreast behind them, the former a little
discomfited that Mrs. Hesseltine had obviously shown him that she preferred her
husband's company to his. Since his rather
depressing *tête-à-tête* with Renée, Huddersfield had not had much conversation with
that lady; indeed she also seemed to avoid
him, so that his visit, so far, had not proved
especially pleasant. Mrs. Gore had spent,
moreover, two days in her room, a prey to
violent neuralgia, and Anthony had been
in an almost lachrymose condition on that
account.

"I can't make out what the deuce is the
matter with her! Bracing air like this ought
to set her up like anything. I do really
believe there's no place like home, nothing
like Crabston after all. I always feel as
fit as a fiddle there, splendid appetite, sleep
like a top, and can take no end of exercise."

Hesseltine had been extremely sympathetic, had sent some of his best champagne to the invalid, and begged she would consider Strathrowan as her own home, and ask for anything and everything that she could possibly fancy. He was much pleased when, on the morning of the day fixed upon for the picnic, Mrs. Gore announced that she was not at all afraid of the fatigue, and would join the party.

The road wound along by the loch, bounded on the other side by a wood of rustling birches, through which a little noisy burn trickled among lichen-covered boulders. The tops of the tallest hills were visible, and every crag on the mountain, where a pair of ospreys yearly made their nest, was sharply pencilled against the soft purple background. Huge tufts of brown bracken grew close to the water's edge, and clusters of rowan-berries formed a vivid spot of colour amid the neutral browns and greens of fern and foliage. The sun poured down blazing beams upon the heads of the pleasure-seekers, who were glad enough when their path led them awhile through a fir-shaded track out of reach of his shafts.

Lord Huddersfield was by this time becoming extremely bored. He cast furtive glances at the two ladies; Renée, in green, on her pony; Léo, in a beautifully-cut plaid skirt, and a "Tam o' Shanter" half hiding her fair curls. He began to feel exasperated with his companions. Lord Strathmashie would do nothing but use strong language about the heat, his eyes half closed, and his voice languid as ever. He was clad in a suit of the "loudest" of checks, to use the slang phraseology to which he was partial, wearing, as Frank told him, "one check only to each leg." Colonel Forester, who owned an inquiring mind, was extremely anxious to know, not only the name of each respective hill, but the shortest cuts to every lodge, the ages of the trees, and the date of construction of the various roads. His constant questionings at last so exasperated Huddersfield, that the latter waited for Frank and his wife to come up, and began walking alongside them instead.

Hesseltine shot a keen quick glance at the young man, and noticed that he seemed a little ill at ease. And then Frank felt curiously annoyed, especially when he also observed that the colour in Léo's face had changed to a deeper pink. He was determined, however, to show the utmost confidence in, and civility to, his guest.

"I think, Léo," he said, "that Mrs. Gore will perhaps like to have some one else to talk to now? I shall walk on and overtake her and Tony. Don't hurry, and make yourself hot and tired."

Huddersfield watched him go with evident satisfaction.

"I was becoming so bored with those

fellows, I could have howled," he said, looking down at the fresh little face beside him.

" I like Lord Strathmashie. He wishes to appear stupid, and succeeds admirably ; but *au fond*, I believe he has a good deal of common sense, and insight into character."

" Which means that he approves and disapproves of the same people that you do, I suppose ? "

" Perhaps it does."

" Well, I am quite indifferent now, thank God, Mrs. Hesseltine, to what the world in general says, or thinks of me."

" So I should have imagined."

" Ah ! but I am *not* indifferent, and never shall be, to what *one* woman thinks. You know only too well whom I mean. To gain her esteem, her forgiveness, I would— I won't say die, because that is banal and commonplace—but I would try and start afresh ; I would endeavour to do some good in what is left to me of my miserable life. Mrs. Hesseltine, do you believe me?"

Léontine's heart began to beat faster, and her limbs shook as she walked.

"It is of no use, you know it as well as I do, to talk to me like this. No, I am not angry, I feel no resentment towards you now. That is all long since a thing of the past. I should be heartily glad, for your *own* sake, if you were to lead a different sort of life. But your path and mine are wide apart for always. I cannot help you more than by wishing you, as an old friend, good and happiness. Let us not talk like this any more."

"You cannot realize in the smallest measure what I feel," said her companion, his voice growing very husky. "You en-slaved me entirely once, and I am still always desirous only to live for you. I will not speak like this any more, though. Forgive me, dear Mrs. Hesseltine, if I pain you. I will be silent, and not trouble you again."

They had reached a stone bridge by a clump of alders, at the further end of which the ponies halted. Léontine had grown pale, and neither the troubled expression on her face, nor the traces of emotion on Huddersfield's, escaped Frank's notice. But he only turned to Mrs. Gore, and bent over her saddle.

"I am afraid this hot ride is too much for you?" he said, kindly.

"Well, I am feeling a little faint. But don't let me bother you, Mr. Hesseltine. You are too good to me."

"I know where there is a small spring close here. The water will be nice and cool; I'll fetch you some." And he started off on the quest.

"My dear child," cried Tony, "you look awfully white! I'll get you a bit of something out of the hamper on that pony.

You must eat a sandwich, Renée, or a slice of chicken."

And he began assiduously fumbling in one of the baskets, with the result that he upset a game-pie into the dust, and broke three glasses and a plate. Frank came back with some fresh water; and a discussion began as to whether Mrs. Gore was well enough to pursue the journey, or no.

" We have three good miles more," said Hesseltine. "Of course when you get up to the loch in the hills, you can rest at the stalker's house. There's a comfortable room enough there. But the question is, whether it wouldn't be wiser for you to go home *now*, and not have the fatigue of the return ride? What do you think, Mrs. Gore? I shall only be too happy to act as your escort!"

At this suggestion Léo's lip quivered with vexation. She was about to speak, when she reflected that Renée might think that she was jealous and annoyed. It would never do to justify such a suspicion.

"I'll take her home," said Anthony. "You're right, Frank, old boy. The ride back 'd be too much for her. That beastly neuralgia pulls one down so. Funny thing, she *never* has it at Crabston!"

"I certainly shan't let you give up the picnic, Tony. Besides, Mrs. Gore has enough of your company all the year round, my dear fellow. I say, hand us a few of the things that you haven't upset, and we'll have our luncheon *en route* homewards. Léo, you'll look after everybody, and see they're not starved?"

His wife did not answer. She felt more pained than she would have cared to own. She merely turned quickly to Lord Huddersfield and said—

"Well, we must try to amuse ourselves as we can," which was rather a foolish observation.

Frank and Mrs. Gore took a homeward course down the winding road, the former saying that he would lead her as much as he could through the trees, so as to avoid the blazing sun.

"I never saw any one so thoughtful as you are, Mr. Hesseltine."

"Well, I have not obeyed your injunctions in one respect, perhaps."

"How do you mean?"

"Don't you remember your caution on your friend's account?"

"Ah! yes, I do indeed. I am afraid it was much needed, poor boy," she sighed.

"Mrs. Gore," said Frank, suddenly, "I want to ask you one question. On the day on which I told you of my engagement, at Ledsham, you said—do you remember it?—that you once feared that my wife would have thrown herself away on some unworthy object? Had that remark of yours any connection with what you have told me here?"

There was a long pause. Renée's eyes were following a pair of bullfinches, whose crimson breasts and white wing-feathers caught the light as they flew. At last she said, slowly and deliberately—

"That is hardly a fair question to ask."

And Frank obtained in this way the information that he wanted.

All the way home, although his companion was charming, bright, and sympathetic, his thoughts were troubled. He began to see, as in a flash of sudden intelligence, that there might have been more reasons than he knew of, to account for the way in which Léontine had at one time repelled him. Then, in his mind's eye, he recalled the staircase at Buckingham Palace, the young Hussar clanking down the steps, and remaining engrossed in conversation with his little Léo. Why had he,

Frank, been so blind? It would have been well if she could have seen that pained expression in his eyes just then, if she had been with him instead of this other woman, and they could have told each other all that was in their hearts, and smiled amid dawning tears, perhaps, at their foolish misunderstandings and fears.

But instead he only heard Renée's low thrilling voice.

"I hate myself for having distressed and worried you; you are such a kind friend."

"Indeed, I am not *a bit* distressed. Why on earth should I be? Every one knows that he is not his wife's first love. He ought only to be grateful, as I am, when he has won a prize coveted by others. Mrs. Gore, shall we sit down under this big fir-tree, and have our luncheon? I suppose the others must be near the loch now." And here he gave a sigh, which, though a faint one, was not lost upon his companion's quick ear.

Meanwhile the rest of the party had toiled slowly up a stony path, winding past crags and huge boulders, till the little lake, sunk deep in the middle of the hills, like a glittering blue precious stone in a velvet case, burst upon their view. Lord Strathmashie unclosed his eyes, and remarked it was "devilish odd how the water got up there," and relapsed into silence again.

The party paused on the shore of the loch, close to a small house occupied by a former stalker of Frank's. It was decided that luncheon should be eaten outside, under a group of fir-trees. Lord Huddersfield, who was decidedly more cheerful than he had been during the previous hours, bustled to and fro with the assiduity of a club waiter; while Colonel Forester, who had learnt about six sentences in Gaelic, embarked, on the strength of that knowledge, in an animated conversation with the stalker's wife.

Léontine was rather more silent than usual. For her the charm of the picnic was gone. Her thoughts followed the two figures whom she had seen gradually disappearing under the fir-boughs, the slender woman in green on her rough pony, and the man who walked by her bridle-rein. Luncheon over, the path by the little loch was explored, and one or two of the men ascended a hill above it to look at the view; Léo, Mrs. Forester, and Lord Huddersfield remaining behind. When the sun had sunk lower behind Strathrowan, and the air grew fresher and more exhilarating, it was decided to begin the homeward walk. Huddersfield joined his hostess, and the two paced silently along side by side.

" You look rather fagged and tired out,

too, Mrs. Hesseltine? Don't you think we might take a shorter cut home?"

"Do you know of one?"

"Yes, I asked the stalker's wife. She said that when we reach the entrance to the fir-wood, we should branch off to the right, instead of to the left. It was on your account I tried to find out, because I thought you seemed as if you had had about enough of it."

"That was very kind of you. I don't really mind which way. Shall we try yours?"

Huddersfield's manner had become so perfectly calm and friendly, that Léontine settled in her own mind that there would be no harm in walking with him now. Perhaps, although she hardly knew it herself, her feeling of vexation with Frank might have had something to say to the resolution. She hesitated, however, still, for an instant.

"I had better tell Mrs. Forester about the short cut too, hadn't I?"

"All right," he answered, with a look of annoyance, which she did not notice. But Colonel Forester, who was not in his own mind perfectly well assured as to the ultimate direction of the road recommended, demurred, after a heated argument of some five minutes.

"If I had a map, now," he said, "it would be well enough. But I can't think that the direct route *can* bear to the right. I see it all in my mind's eye. *Your* path slopes away, past the burn, and that little clump of mountain-ashes. Then you have that queer-shaped boulder, like a crouching dog, facing you, a little to the east. *I* should say—"

Lord Strathmashie here yawned so loud that the Colonel stopped abruptly, with a rather fierce look at that gentleman through his eyeglass.

"Well," said Huddersfield, "I think Mrs. Hesseltine and I will trust Mrs. MacIver, and leave you to the more circuitous course. We shall all meet safely at the end, let us hope."

He and Léontine turned off under the dark stretch of wood, waving their hands to the group behind them.

A perfect colony of bullfinches seemed to be flitting among the boughs, and here and there a little yellow siskin flew from one fir-branch to another, twittering as he went. Enormous scarlet fungi grew upon the path, among dried cones and slippery fir-branches. Outside the wood lay a stretch of moor, with a narrow path alongside a foaming burn. Léo stopped for an instant to see the amber-coloured waves dashing and hurling themselves to pieces on the rocks. The lowering sun cast a scarlet glow over the stems at the opening of another wood.

" Which is our way now ? "

" Straight on down the path, and through this little belt of trees. Then we come on to the open ground again, and through one more wood, till we find a wider road leading to your own loch. You see Mrs. MacIver was quite right. We shall have saved a good mile and a half."

He stopped suddenly, plucked a bit of white heather, and handed it to Léo.

" A good omen, isn't it, for our walk? That means luck to you and to me. Shall I pin it in your dress for you ? "

" No, thanks, you keep it, as you discovered the treasure. I *am* lucky enough already, Lord Huddersfield, you see. I don't want anything more."

He turned sharply away, and said nothing until they reached the belt of the trees. Then when they came into the dimmer light under the boughs, he observed—

" It was very good of you to take this

walk with me. This is the only pleasant time I have had for months and months past."

Léontine impatiently struck at a scarlet fungus with her stick, till it lay bruised and crumbling across her path. She did not answer the above remark.

They came out on to the heather again, but this time no direct track seemed to be visible. Huddersfield cast his eye along a line of boulders.

"I'm afraid it will be roughish walking here," he said.

"There does not seem to be any pathway! You must have made a mistake! And the wood beyond seems ever so much wider and thicker than the others we have passed!"

"It will be all right," he answered. "I suppose there is no use in my offering you a hand over these rough stones and clumps of heather? Be careful, then, that you don't sprain your foot."

Léontine, with rising colour, stumbled over a bit of rock in her hurry to get on, and saved herself from falling by digging her stick into the ground. They scrambled on as best they could, and there was certainly no semblance now of any path; the ground sloping as they went towards the wood.

"Look out!" shouted the young man. "I have just stepped into a sort of bog. Stay where you are. I'll collect some stones, and make a bridge for you."

He fetched two or three fragments of rock, and on these rather rickety stepping-stones, Léontine crossed the wet ground and came into the wood. The pathway in front, a very narrow one, seemed endless, a dark passage with no friendly light beyond. Léontine's heart sank, but she redoubled her pace, and walked on in front of her companion. A suspicion, which she tried to repel, dawned upon her

that he had brought her this way on
purpose to prolong, instead of to shorten,
their time together. At last, after many
windings, a glimmer of blue distance shone
into the sombre aisle.

"There's the moor!" cried Huddersfield.
"Now we've only got to cut across it, and
we shall get straight out into the broad
road by the loch. I fear good Mrs. Mac
Iver mistook the distances, though, after all."

The sun was very low when they reached
the heather again, and once more there
was no trace of a beaten route, or of
a road beyond. Huddersfield stood still,
straining his eyes over the moor. The
air was calm and still, and a red glow shone
upon his face and fair hair. Léontine,
more tired than she would have cared
to acknowledge, sat down upon a fragment
of rock. She certainly did not wish to
appeal to him for sympathy in her fatigue,
and her heart was swelling with indignation.

"The others will be home *hours* before us!" she said, with quivering lips.

"No, no; indeed they won't! We are all right, Mrs. Hesseltine. We must cross the heather here, and we are simply *bound* to reach the road. It lies low, that's why I can't see it yet."

She rose, and followed him over the barren moorland, stumbling now more than ever since she had become so wearied. A little bird, uttering a cry of pain and fear, darted across the air in front of her. Léo saw his enemy, a sparrow-hawk, hovering above him, and she turned sick as he swooped upon the helpless small creature and seized him in his cruel talons. On she went, dragging her feet one after the other, her back aching, her limbs growing stiff. Suddenly she saw that they would have to cross another burn, or take a circuitous course back again over the moor. It was a wide stream with steep banks.

"I'm awfully sorry," said Huddersfield. "I only wish you'd let me carry you over?"

"Certainly not, thanks; I can manage to cross by those two big stones."

Gathering her skirt a little higher, and planting her stick on the ground, Léo slowly descended. The ground was softer here than she had expected; one stone slid away under her foot, and she fell, striking her shoulder against a large jutting rock.

Huddersfield, who was in front, heard a low cry of pain, and saw her lying prostrate beneath the bank, her skirt draggling in the water, her red cap fallen off her fair curls. In one second he was beside her, and had lifted her across the stream. Then she roused herself, but her face was deadly white.

"I think my arm is broken," she said, in a faint voice. "I feel dreadfully exhausted. Leave me quiet for a few minutes. . . I will try presently to go on. . ."

Huddersfield drew out a flask of whiskey from his pocket, and she drank a little. He felt the arm very gently. Then he took his walking-stick, and with his powerful arms snapped it in two.

"I will tie your arm up to this. Give me your handkerchief."

She handed it to him, and Huddersfield skilfully fastened the injured arm to this extemporary splint.

"Lean on me," he said, very tenderly. "I am more cut up than I can say to see you so hurt, and you're so awfully plucky. We will soon be over the moor now."

Very slowly the pair crossed the heather in the growing darkness; Léontine silent and deadly pale, Huddersfield's heart beating as he looked at her and led her gently along. The broad road was reached at last, and then, in spite of the darkness,

Léontine, faint with fatigue and pain, sank down by one of the milestones. The stars were beginning to twinkle over the loch. A few birds rustled in the boughs, agitated by the sound of steps and voices.

Huddersfield looked hopelessly round him. The nearest lodge was four miles away, Strathrowan itself at least three. To his intense joy a distant sound of wheels fell upon his ear, drawing nearer and nearer. It was a dog-cart, containing two of Hesseltine's men, on their way to Strathrowan. In a few minutes Léontine had been helped into the cart, and in twenty minutes the lights of the Castle were close to her. But her eyes were closed, and she was insensible from pain and exhaustion when they lifted her out, and carried her into the hall.

# CHAPTER VII.

THE Foresters, Lord Strathmashie, and the others who had joined the picnic arrived at Strathrowan before sunset. Hesseltine and Mrs. Gore, now apparently entirely recovered from her past fatigues, came out to meet them. Frank's eye took in the group with one quick glance, and a very slight frown, so little a one that it was merely a passing shadow of displeasure, crossed his brow.

"Where is Léo?" he asked.

"Coming, or rather ought to be come!" said Anthony, his square face lighting up pleasantly when he saw his wife.

"How do you mean?"

"They took," explained Colonel Forester, "what they considered a short cut. But I fear that that very intelligent woman, the wife of your late stalker, Mrs. MacIver, was wrong. I said, didn't I?"—with a triumphant glance round—"that I could not see how a direct route could bear to the right? You remember what I told them? 'Your path,' I said, 'slopes away past the burn. Then you have that queer-shaped boulder—'"

"I suppose they'll be here, anyhow, directly," said Frank, a little impatiently.

"Poor Léo, how tired she'll be!" Renée murmured in her gentle voice. "It was not very wise to trust to a short cut. I never should do so in a country like this!"

Frank was standing out on the path, straining his eyes up the winding road. There was no sign of any approaching figures. He felt rather inclined to be cross at Anthony's exuberant cheerfulness.

"We missed you awfully, you two. But we had a ripping day all the same, and such a lunch! I congratulate you, Frank, on that game-pie. We'd a splendid view of the country, too; at least we energetic chaps who weren't afraid of being blown. That lazy Huddersfield stopped behind, though, with Mrs. Hesseltine. The walk would have done him good—kept his weight down. Well, Renée, my dear old child, you look quite bobbish again."

And he pinched her ear, a habit which always irritated his wife, whose expression of countenance had already more of a sneer than a smile in it. Lord Strathmashie also looked annoyed; but he did not express his feelings more than by giving a very curt answer to a question of Mrs. Gore's. When that lady had gone into the drawing-room, accompanied by Frank, he suddenly turned to Mrs. Forester, and pointed with his thumb to Renée's retreating form.

"Like that woman?" he said, laconically.

"Do you mean Mrs. Gore? Well, I've not had much chance of judging. Of course in her own line she's very handsome; but I think her face rather hard."

"There's something a little sketchy about her, in my opinion," replied Lord Strath-mashie. "My advice to you and all other Johnnies is, 'Don't you trust her much further than you see her.'"

And he looked languidly at the sunset, while Mrs. Forester laughed.

"Well, I hope at least you admire Mrs. Hesseltine without any reservations? To my mind it is the sweetest little face I ever saw."

"*She's* a clinker," said Strathmashie, slowly and impressively, and thereupon strolled into the billiard-room.

Renée sat down at the piano, and sang

song after song, by heart, to her host and
Anthony, and the stars came out one by
one while she sang. Hesseltine, with a
very sad look in his eyes, watched the mass
of smoky cloud lying on the horizon, sur-
mounted by a lake of fire, until the scarlet
changed to orange, and the orange to
primrose colour. Two or three labouring
men going home by the loch showed as
black silhouettes against the fiery background. The water seemed almost asleep ;
the plashing of the tiny wavelets was
scarcely audible. He could not account for
the dull heartache which he felt as he
looked out upon the evening peace of the
Highland landscape. Why did he mentally
confound it with another view from a place
a long way off and totally unlike it ? The
purple hills seemed to sink into stretches
of green vineyard, the loch gradually to
contract into a flowing river. Surely there
was a scent of dead rose-leaves in the room,

instead of the fresh flowers that Léo had arranged only yesterday? Now she seemed to stand before him, a little older and sadder, but with the same face. What was the unspoken tragedy that lurked in her eyes and her sweet mouth?

"What a fool I am!" thought Hesseltine, while the sound of Renée's voice singing seemed to belong to some other sphere. "A morbid fool! Why should I, of all men, be gloomy and suspicious? Nothing has happened, nothing to change the happiness which fate has bestowed. When I get low like this, I only want some experienced sensible friend to cheer me up—a friend such as Charley was. Dear old boy! Does he know, I wonder, that his child is here with me? that I would give my very soul, I believe, to make her life bright? But shall I? Don't we all fail to do the very things we are most bent upon carrying out? Supposing—supposing that she is not happy after all? It's very early to fail, and God knows I've done the best I could."

"Renée, let us have something more cheerful! It's enough to give one the dumps the way you go on singing about death, and forsaken lovers, and all those kind of things."

Anthony was leaning on the piano, his large red hands aimlessly turning over pieces of music.

"Well, what shall I sing? Mr. Hesseltine, what would *you* like?"

Frank started. He was ashamed to realize how little his brain had taken in either of words or music.

"Sing me ' My faithful Johnnie.' That's a great favourite of mine."

"Yes," said Anthony; "it's a bit more cheery than most of 'em. That pair get all right at last, I suppose. But women like sentiment. I say, it's getting pretty dark—I'll light the candles."

He caught his foot in the music-stool,
saved himself by seizing the piano and
making the strings shake violently, and
proceeded to illuminate the room.

The dressing-gong sounded; but there
was still no sign of the wanderers. Frank
was obviously so worried when they sat
down to dinner, that Renée thought it
wiser to leave him alone. Once she asked
if he had sent any one to see where Léontine
and Lord Huddersfield could be?

"Yes, of course I have. Hallo! there's
a door-bell!"

He sprang up, and ran out into the hall,
followed by several of his guests. Léontine
was being carried up the steps, followed by
Huddersfield, who looked pale and much
worried. In a few words he related what
had happened; but Hesseltine did not re-
ceive the explanation with much cordiality.

"I can't imagine why, in Heaven's name,
you should go on a sort of wild-goose chase

over a country you don't know, or why
you should invite my wife to accompany
you on it. She is not so particularly strong,
and the fall may have shaken her very
much. Johnson, send off at once for Dr.
MacDougall. You all go on, please, with
dinner; don't wait for me."

He followed his wife up-stairs. A few
minutes after they had laid her on the bed
she opened her eyes. Her husband bent
over her.

"I am afraid your arm is very painful,
Léo?"

Although she was still half dazed, the
coldness of his voice struck her disagreeably,
and she resented it.

"Of course it hurts me a good deal."

"Why on earth did you run all over the
country in that foolish way? Huddersfield
ought to have known better than to advise
you to go."

Her cheeks, just before so white, crimsoned

under Frank's gaze, which was not a very sympathetic one, considering that she was suffering much.

" I don't know," she stammered, her face growing hotter.

" Perhaps he wanted to prolong the walk with you ! "

The moment Frank had spoken he wished the words unsaid.

" Never mind, Léo, don't worry now. You must try to get to sleep. Don't bother yourself. It can't be undone now."

The tears were welling into her eyes. It was such a different reception from the one that she had expected to meet, and she was feeling very ill and worn-out. There was a light tapping at the door, and a brilliant face, with rosy cheeks, looked in.

" I've only just come to ask if I can be of the least use ? I am very good with sick people."

" *How* kind of you, Mrs. Gore ! But

you ought not to have hurried up from dinner. It's just like you, though. No, thanks so much; I think the only thing for Léo now is complete rest. And she's got a very devoted maid to look after her."

Léontine noticed the cordiality of his voice, and for one moment she almost hated this obliging Mrs. Gore. She buried her fair curly head among the pillows and made no reply.

"Léontine, I think you might thank Mrs. Gore."

The girl turned impatiently on her bed.

"I am so tired, Frank; forgive me if I forget my manners."

His heart smote him, and he bent down and kissed her.

"Poor little woman! Well, you must try and sleep. I'll send Marie in at once. I hope you'll be freer from all this pain and discomfort to-morrow."

She raised her lips to his; but there was

a choking sensation in her throat, and she could not speak. She was tired and over-wrought, and a despairing feeling had crept into her heart, which had deepened when she heard the very friendly way in which her husband had spoken to Renée. She was becoming intensely jealous of this beautiful woman, with her dark, observant eyes and furtive smile, wounded to the quick at a fear which would obtrude itself, that Frank was evidently beginning to take too much pleasure in Mrs. Gore's society. Had Léo been less physically suffering, she might more easily have shaken off these gnawing doubts; but the result of them was that she passed a restless and feverish night, and looked so ill on the following morning that Hesseltine became alarmed. The doctor, however, gave a fairly reassuring report. Rest, and freedom from worry, he said, would soon restore her.

Mrs. Gore, meanwhile, had consulted

with her husband as to whether it was not better to go back to England.

"You know best, old girl, you always do," was his answer.

And Renée thereupon sought Mr. Hesseltine in his sitting-room, and announced their attention of leaving for the south.

"Please do nothing of the kind," said Frank. "Think of my solitary meals, for Strathmashie is obliged to go. You will really do me a kindness if you stay, and Tony will enjoy a few more days on the hill. Huddersfield came in just now, and he is starting off to-night."

"Well, if you seriously and truly wish it, of course we'll stay. And you'll let me know if Léo would care for me to go and read to her, or to sing to her, if she likes?"

Lord Strathmashie, who was smoking in the garden, passed the window and looked in.

"That woman is playing the devil," he

soliloquized, as he walked up and down.
Presently he too came into Frank's sitting-
room.

"I say, old boy," he said.   "Mrs. Hesseltine said something the other day about
wanting a poetry-book by Morris, I think
the fellow's name is.   I sent for it for her,
and it's in my room.   Just you give it her,
will you, from me, with my very best
regards, as a little farewell offering?"

"Certainly," said Frank, looking rather
amused.   "I'm very sorry you're off, old
chap; but the Gores are kindly staying on
to keep me company."

"Are they?   I should call her a limpet,
always clinging on where she can."

"I may just remark, my dear boy, I
*asked* them to stay."

"Of course, an Englishman's house is his
castle," said the other, a little vaguely.
"Odd woman, Mrs. Gore; reminds me of
a leopard, way she walks round and looks

at you, as if she was going to spring. Well,
I won't bother you now any more. I'll
leave that old book outside, and don't forget
my message to Mrs. Hesseltine."

Lord Strathmashie had certainly become
more conversational of late; in fact this
last was about the longest sentence of which
he had ever been known to deliver himself.
Frank went on with his letters, but from
time to time he laid down his pen, and
remained idle for a few minutes, blankly
staring out at the garden, and the glimmer
of water through the trees. A servant
brought in a telegram, and on opening it
Frank's ejaculation was hardly flattering to
the sender. It ran—

"Leaving soon for south. May we come
Saturday to Tuesday? Please wire, Lady
Mary Prosser."

"What an infernal nuisance!" said
Frank aloud. He mentally added: "But
I suppose I must answer the usual lie—

'delighted to see you.' Here, James, take this up to Mrs. Hesseltine's room."

Léontine, however, was not at all annoyed at the idea of Lady Mary's arrival, as she thought that it might perhaps prevent so many confidential interviews between her husband and Renée. She sent a message down to Frank that she would be very pleased to see the Prossers; and shortly afterwards her husband came into the room, with rather a cloudy brow.

" It's the greatest bore that the Prossers are coming, isn't it?" he said. "But I never would refuse to see her, for Charley Marsham's sake."

The large violet eyes, which were so like poor Charley's own, rested anxiously on him.

" I am so sorry, Frank, that you will be bothered. But I am much better, and shall be able to entertain Lady Mary. Oh, please, thank Lord Strathmashie very much

for the book. And Lord Huddersfield"—
here she took up a note in her little white
fingers—"has written me such a kind letter,
wishing me good-bye. Will you read it?"

It is well known that people who are
inclined to blush change colour much more
frequently when they are weak and exhausted. Léo's cheeks were crimson as she
finished her sentence.

"Oh, thanks, I don't know that it's
worth reading. I owe him a grudge for
letting you break your arm, and knocking
you up."

"It was not his fault about the arm,"
cried Léo, colouring still more vividly.

"Well, we needn't discuss whose fault it
was, my child." He stooped and kissed her
on the forehead.

Léo threw her uninjured arm round his
neck.

"Dear old Frank, will you stay and read
to me?"

He hesitated.

"I would certainly, but I promised Mrs. Gore to give her another lesson with her rifle."

"Can't she wait?" and Léo's lip quivered. "I am so sick of the Gores, I wish they were gone!"

"You are very unreasonable, Léo. She has been awfully kind, wanting to come and look after you."

"I am tired of seeing her. She will never be a great friend of mine. Some people may like her immensely, but she isn't sympathetic to me."

Frank looked quickly at Léo, whose eyes were sparkling.

"Some people do admire her enormously," he replied in a quiet voice, and walked across to the window. A stab of pain had run through his heart. Doubtless Léontine knew that Mrs. Gore was an old and intimate friend of Lord Huddersfield's,

and therefore she was, although she perhaps did not herself know it, jealous of
Renée.

"Well," he said after a pause, "I'll
come back and read to you later on, dear.
Shall it be a novel, or a newspaper, or
what?"

"I don't want to be read to at all, if you
cannot stop with me now!"

Hesseltine was provoked at her petulance,
all the more so as he wrongly suspected its
source. He did not go and kiss her again,
but went straight out of the room, and
found Renée Gore, radiant and smiling,
awaiting him in her walking-dress.

Léontine, meanwhile, was tossing rest-
lessly on the bed, trying to keep back her
tears.

"Why, why does he leave me when I'm
ill, for that woman? I know she likes him,
and she cannot bear me. She will take
him away from me, because she is older,

and cleverer, and is handsomer, and knows
more."

The German maid came gently into the
room, and bent over the bed. The sound
of her beloved native language seemed to
soothe the poor child.

"Madame looks so tired. She must
really try and get some sleep. The room
shall be darkened, and that will rest her."

Léontine allowed her faithful Marie to
shake her pillows, and put eau-de-Cologne
on her head. And shortly afterwards she
fell into a troubled sleep. Meanwhile
Frank was giving his painstaking and
charming pupil a long lesson with her rifle.

Lord Strathmashie took his departure on
the following morning. The air was fresh
and cold as he crossed the loch in the little
boat, and the sky rosy, the early morning
light twinkling on the window-panes of the
invalid's room. Anthony Gore had accompanied him to get, as he said, "a bit of a

walk, from the first stage where the coach was to change horses."

" You'll pick up a flea or two, if ther're many collie dogs on the coach," said his lordship. " How long, by the way, do you sponge on here, Anthony ? "

" Oh, I think for the inside of a week, or so, more. I've had a rattling good time ; I've got, let me see—"

" Don't, for heaven's sake, tell me how many stags in the last ten years, and all the weights," said the other, with a yawn. " Here we are, and I think I hear this rotten old coach coming. Jolly pink sky, over the Castle. Wish I was stopping on. Good-bye, Donald ; " and a handsome gratuity placed in the boatman's hand caused a smile to creep almost up to his high cheek-bones.

On Saturday the Claggan coach bore upon its box-seat no less distinguished a person than Mr. Prosser, Q.C., M.P. for the

Muddiford Boroughs. The driver and a shepherd exchanged winks at the sight of his portly figure in his kilt, in which he certainly did not yet appear perfectly at home. During the drive the eminent politician and the coachman discussed the Crofter Question, the Free and Established Churches, and the advantages and disadvantages of large deer-forests, such as the one for which he was bound. Lady Mary, who was suffering from one of her heavy colds, was inside, in company with her maid, Josephine ; an old man in a plaid, who changed his wet shoes and stockings in her presence, to her unbounded disgust ; a stout woman with a parcel of dried haddocks ; a small boy in a highland bonnet, who ate malodorous sugar-plums ; and two sheep-dogs with dirty coats. She was not sorry when the drive of over twenty miles came to an end.

That evening, Léontine, lying on her sofa,

received a visit from Lady Mary. After a
good deal of varied conversation, the latter
said—

"I think, dear Mrs. Hesseltine, if I were
you, I would not make a *great* friend of
Mrs. Gore."

The brilliant eyes, so deep and so blue,
looked anxiously up at Lady Mary.

"I am not likely to do so. I don't much
care for her, though she has always been
nice and kind to me. Frank is a very old
friend of Mr. Gore's, and that is really why
they are here."

"Well, I have heard she was considered
rather fast, and curious, as a girl. When
my cousin was ambassador in Paris, he
knew the Morants. I fancy she was a good
deal talked about."

"I don't know much about her really,"
said Léo, sighing wearily, and stretching
her sound arm over her head. "Frank
says she is a most devoted daughter,

and that she is charming in her own
house."

Lady Mary's pursed-up lips looked as if
they longed to say more, but on the whole
considered silence the better part. That
evening, when alone with Mr. Prosser, she
discoursed at some length upon Mrs. Gore
and her peculiarities.

"Did it not strike you, Daniel, that she
made up a great deal to Mr. Hesseltine?
I don't approve of that way she has
of glancing up at people under her
eyelids."

Lady Mary's own prominent light orbs
were fixed anxiously on her Q.C. Mr.
Prosser had been honestly too much struck
by the handiwork of Frank's *chef* to bestow
much attention upon the sphinx-like Mrs.
Gore. He folded his hands across his
stomach, his favourite attitude; and looked
first at the fire, then at Lady Mary, who
had on, as usual, a mustard - coloured

dressing-gown, considering this to be a good wearing colour.

"I have the greatest opinion of your powers of observation, my dearest Mary. They are seldom, if ever, at fault. It would be well perhaps to hint discreetly to poor Mrs. Hesseltine that her guests have stayed long enough. You have such tact, dear child, that you will do this in a way that will not wound her, I have no doubt." And with his fat hand, on which a diamond ring sparkled, he patted Lady Mary's thin red fingers approvingly.

Léontine came down-stairs two days before the departure of the Anthony Gores. She was honestly a little tired of her *téte-à-tétes* in her room with Lady Mary, full as they always were of much good advice; and more anxious than she would have cared to own, to see if there was really much foundation for her dawning fears about her husband's liking for Renée. It was unfor-

tunate that just as she came into the
drawing-room, her arm encased in plaster
of Paris, her face white and drawn, she
should see Frank and Mrs. Gore coming
homewards together over the hill, laughing
and talking merrily. Lady Mary, who was
employed upon an abnormally hideous
worsted fender-stool, looked up and observed—

" Mrs. Gore seems to be very fond of long
walks, especially if she can get the society
of some gentleman all to herself ! "

Anthony burst into the room.

"Awfully glad to see you down, Mrs.
Hesseltine ! Well done, you ! You look
a bit white and seedy, though. We've
missed you a lot, but my girl has done her
best to keep us all cheerful. Here's a
telegram for you."

It was a message from Lord Huddersfield,
expressing a hope that Mrs. Hesseltine was
really much better. As she was reading

it, Frank and Mrs. Gore came into the room.

"Well, my little Léo, this is nice! I am so glad to see you down again!" He came towards his wife. "Who's the wire from? Ah! Huddersfield."

He glanced at the paper, but scarcely read a word beyond the signature, and his manner changed a little.

"You must answer it," he said a little brusquely. "The reply's paid."

"*You* answer it for me, Frank!"

"Oh no, it's to *you*. Mrs. Gore, what do you say to piquet before tea? I must have my revenge."

Léontine's colour rose. She took a pencil and wrote—"It is most kind of you to think of me. I am getting well, very many thanks." She hesitated, and added—"Hope we shall see you in London," and handed the message to a servant who came in with a basket of peats. Lady Mary's

figure, clad in a gown of brown cashmere
with magenta spots, rose from a seat in the
window.

"Shall we play backgammon, Léo? Or
will you wait for Daniel? It is his favourite
game."

"I am too tired to play anything, thank
you," said Léontine, and she lay back in her
deep chair, while Frank moved his card-
table nearer the fire. She kept her eyes
closed for some time, but now and then
they would open against her will, to watch
the piquet players. Renée, sometimes
absorbed in her cards, sometimes with that
triumphant smile that Léontine was beginning to detest, playing round the corners of
her mouth; Frank, pre-occupied with the
game.

Anthony came in, with a loud banging of
doors, and an unmelodious whistle, and
began to read extracts from *Punch* aloud,
to the annoyance of all present. Lady

Mary occasionally looked up from her worsted-work, and at last felt impelled to give a little good advice.

"I'm sure, Léo, you've forgotten your tonic! I wish you would take Dr. Dobson Bruce's prescription instead. It quite set mamma up this last summer."

Léontine said she would go up-stairs and lie down—she almost felt inclined to add, like a petulant child, because she was evidently not wanted here. About half an hour afterwards Frank found her, stretched on a sofa and sobbing bitterly. The sight of her little tearful face, with swollen eyes and nostrils, cut him to the heart.

"What's the matter, my darling? Are you in pain? Why didn't you send for me?"

She covered her face with her hands, and more tears ran through them. Frank put his arm tenderly round her.

"My child, my dear little Léo, do tell me

what it is? I thought you were much better."

There was no answer, but more choking sobs. Frank drew her closer into his arms.

" I can't say anything to comfort you, if I don't know what's the matter."

" Nothing, nothing, I am only so tired, and I felt lonely and miserable."

He started, and his arms loosened their hold ever so little.

" Why should you feel lonely?" She went on crying still more vehemently. How could she say, Because you played piquet with Mrs. Gore instead of talking to me? Because you walked with her this afternoon? No, that was impossible. Even to herself Léo would hardly own that she was afraid that another woman would supplant her in her husband's love; to himself it was still more difficult to hint at such a grief. And he, for his part, began

to imagine that her sorrow and loneliness
were connected with the departure of the
man whom she had formerly loved—yes,
better than himself. He felt a tightening
at his heart. He was not sure if he were
angry with her, or only with himself for his
own stupidity. Yet he surely loved her
more tenderly than ever. He made one
more effort.

"My dear little Léo, be reasonable!
What do you want me to do? Would
you care to ask any one else here to be
with you?"

"No, no, no!"

"Well, what can I do? Mrs. Gore said
she was sure your nerves were shaken by
the accident. That is why you are so
overcome now, about—nothing?"

She turned her head away.

"Mrs. Gore knows nothing about me,"
she said shortly.

"I can't make out why you should speak

in such an antagonistic way about her. It's a new departure, you never did in London. It's only since they came here!"

"I am sick of the very sound of her name!"

"I have told them, though, that we will go and stay at Crabston. Darling Léo, *do* try not to be so cross!"

For all answer, she began to cry again more bitterly; and Frank, whose temper was, as we know, an impatient one, spoke more sharply to her than he had ever done since his marriage.

"I do wish to goodness you would control yourself—not go into these foolish hysterics about nothing! If your arm hurt you, I should be sorry, but I cannot pity a person who cries like a cross child for no reason!"

He went out of the room, banging the door after him. Léo, to whom his tone came as a sort of shock, remained almost stupefied. Could this be Frank, the lover whose tenderness had wrapped her round during all the months of their married life, who had never spoken a harsh word to her, who had seemed to live only to give her pleasure? She lay shivering and miserable in her fast-darkening room. And ever and anon, Renée's face would obtrude itself. It seemed to come between her and Frank's— triumphant, smiling, brilliant.

Hesseltine himself, thoroughly remorseful at his impatience, shut himself gloomily into his own sitting-room. With arms resting on his writing-table, he looked up at Charley Marsham's picture.

"How many of my friends have had their lives spoilt by a woman!" he thought.

> "'Oh! World of ours, are you so grey,
> And weary, World, of spinning,
> That you repeat the tales to-day
> You told at the beginning?'

"How true that verse is! Why was I to expect I should be more lucky than all the rest ? Poor little child ! it isn't her *fault*, after all, if she likes that fellow best. There is not much in me to win a woman's love."

And up-stairs Léontine was lying with aching head and burning cheeks—sobbing forlornly, as she thought of a past June in a garden of roses, far away in her own Rhineland.

# CHAPTER VIII.

MR. MORANT had only let his house among the firs for the summer months; and December found him installed there again, together with his daughter, who was paying a long visit, and Nanny, and little Jos.

Renée and her father were sitting over a fire of logs one Sunday afternoon, entirely happy in each other's society. A distant ringing of church-bells gave an impression of peace and quiet English home-life. She had walked over the moor that morning with Jos, and listened, outwardly patient,

at least, to forty minutes of good advice
from a mild curate, who looked about
eighteen. She would not, on any account,
have set a bad example in church to Jos,
who, for his part, had found great difficulty
in keeping his eyes open, until he discovered
a live robin hopping to and fro from a
monument to the lectern, which pleased
him much. He was now employed in
building a church of bricks, of an unknown
order of architecture, under Nanny's super-
vision up-stairs.

"I think," said Mr. Morant suddenly,
"that Lord Huddersfield has been over here
quite often enough."

"What makes you say that, *à propos* of
nothing, darling?"

"Well, I've been thinking it over. He
has been here twice to dinner, which is
expensive, as he drinks so much champagne,
at least three times to luncheon, besides
other days in the afternoon."

" He is going soon to India, I believe. He thinks of giving up his staff appointment."

" Well, that won't be a bad thing."

" You used to like Lord Huddersfield, father ? "

" Pretty well. He is not the type of man that I prefer."

" He is a little more entertaining than your son-in-law, at any rate, dear."

" Renée, it is foolish to talk like that."

" Well, when wasn't I foolish ? I'm going up now, however, to read to Nanny, as she has caught a chill, and can't go to church. We shall have a sharp frost to-night. My fingers ache with the cold."

She ran up-stairs, kissed the faithful nurse impetuously, and offered to read her anything that she wished. Nanny chose her favourite chapters, the two last in the Bible, and Renée opened the large book, in which were various inscriptions and pathetic little relics, collected by the old woman. There was the date of Mrs. Gore's birth, and her brother's—father of little Jos— also those of Mrs. Morant's death, and of another brother of Renée's who had died in infancy. Dried flowers lurked between the pages, and funeral cards with more or less sombre edges were carefully stuck upon every vacant space. Within was also an elaborately embroidered book-marker, made by Renée when she was a little girl, frayed at the edges now and a good deal thumbed.

Nanny fixed adoring eyes on her young lady—the being whom she loved best in all the world—as Mrs. Gore sat down and opened the heavy book. To the old nurse the latter was always " Miss Renée," the spoilt child, often naughty, but full of good resolves and tender impulses; who, if she said flippant and heartless things, did not really mean them ; who was always ready to

give up a day's pleasure to amuse her sick
father or her faithful Nanny.

And Renée's sweet thrilling voice lingered
over the poetry and pathos of the wonderful
words, which the veriest sceptic can surely
hardly read and remain unmoved. She
told of the city of pure gold like unto clear
glass; of the glittering jewels, rosy and
green, amber and violet, of which its foundations were built; of the tree with its
healing leaves, and the river shining like
crystal as it flowed. Better than all, of the
light brighter than candle or sun, of the
faces that will be tearless, the tired souls
who will rest at last. All that was of good
and of God in her seemed to start into
being as she read. Her face glowed with
intense appreciation of the word-picture of
this mystic city; her eyes and lips grew
soft as when she was a little child, and had
listened to these same words at the knees of
the mother who was now perhaps a witness

of that glory.   And when she had shut the book and looked up at Nanny's patient face—waiting awhile, poor trusting soul, in patient expectation that such visions of gladness would soon be hers—Renée's tears, which she could not hold back, dropped down fast upon the worn leather binding.

"Oh, Nanny, if I were only a little girl again!   If I could feel that I was not shut out!"

"What do you mean, dearie, what is it, Miss Renée?"   And the wrinkled hand of the old nurse rested lovingly on the girl's head.   "What are you crying for, darling? Well, well, sure enough the words do make one rather choky. Often as I've heard them I still feel a bit upset over 'em to-day.   But it ain't really anything to cry for.   Think of your dear mamma up there, and your little brother, and of how happy we'll all be."

Renée's dark head, and her beautiful

face, so proud and passionate, were buried upon Nanny's black alpaca-covered shoulder. Jos, who had been relegated to the night nursery, looked in, rather puzzled.

"I've done the church, and now, Aunt Renée," he said, "I've made a barracks, and I've put Mr. Noah out as an officer, and one of his sons as sentry. Come and see."

She lifted her head, dried her wet eyes, and laughed.

"All right, old man. But I mustn't leave grandpapa alone any more. If you will be good, and play quietly, you may come down too."

That evening Renée Gore read a letter from Lord Huddersfield attentively, over and over again. He begged for another interview before long, his movements being, so he said, very uncertain. He really was tremendously anxious to see her, more than she believed. He often thought of their last walk in the dusk down the fir-wood, etc., etc., etc.

Renée drew out a sheet of writing-paper, and wrinkled her fair forehead in some perplexity.

At last she wrote, " I am afraid I can't very well ask you *here*. My father thinks you have been already much too often. I will go by train on Tuesday at about four o'clock to Widhurst station. That is close to the Barley Mow Inn. I will meet you there, and we can have five-o'clock-tea and a talk. I shall return by train, I am not afraid of travelling in the dark. *À bientôt* —RENÉE."

Alas! for the change in the face of the woman who carefully sealed this letter. It was no longer the same one that had melted and softened scarcely an hour ago over some inspired words ; it was the face of one much older, harder, and sin-stained. Her dead mother, who had left her long ago, would

surely have known her again as she bent
over the divine book ; but as certainly not
now. All the grace of innocent childhood
had fled, and the tender light in her eyes
had died in dimness and gloom.

*    *    *    *    *

A young lady, very spruce and well-
dressed, got out at the little station of
Widhurst, and walked swiftly up the road
leading to the Barley Mow Inn. This
respectable tavern looked cheerful enough,
even on a gray December day, when damp
still hung in the air, and a watery sun
struggled feebly over the opposite fields.
Sitting at the bow window of the best
private sitting-room, Renée took off her hat
and gloves, and looked out through the
rather dim panes. Across the road was a
high hedge full of the plant familiarly
known as "old man's beard," and on the
fluffy white tufts dew-drops glistened
abundantly. The sun made a praiseworthy

attempt to shine on a ploughed field by the
railway-line, and lit up the white under-
feathers of hundreds of plovers hovering over
it. The poultry, in the yard behind the inn,
cackled contentedly; and a maid in the
lower regions began to sing, not untunefully,
the first verse of a popular sentimental
ballad. Renée looked at the clock, which
marked the time as a quarter-past four.

"Ah!" she thought, "that clever *Com-
tesse Diane* says, 'On arrive en avance,
a l'heure juste, ou en retard, selon qu'on
aime, qu'on aime encore, ou qu'on n'aime
plus.' But that can't be true of him! If
I were only sure that he would never come
under Léo Hesseltine's influence again, I
should not be afraid. The more she repels
him the more anxious he will be to win her
affection. Like a fool, I have never con-
cealed my own feelings from him. Had I
done so, he might have felt for me what he
does for *her*."

Renée rose and rang the bell.

"Is not the tea ready? I ordered it when I came in."

"Directly, madam," answered an awe-struck maid, looking admiringly at Renée's tall form and dazzling skin. "There's tea-cakes and plum-buns, and fresh eggs too, if you like them?"

"All right, only make haste, I am so tired."

Once more she looked through the misty panes, and suddenly the vivid pink of her cheeks paled a little. Huddersfield, mounted on a chestnut pony, was trotting slowly towards the inn. He dismounted, sent the animal round to the stables, and she heard his voice in the entrance.

"Is there a room up-stairs, a private room, where I can have a cup of tea?"

"Well, sir, there *is* a private room, least-ways there *was*, but there's a lady up there now."

"Oh, I dare say she won't mind."

"Elizabeth, show the gentleman to No. 14."

And his steps came nearer. The door of No. 14 being thrown open, Lord Huddersfield, in the most surprised and coolly-friendly manner that he could assume, exclaimed—

"This is really too funny our meeting here, of all places! I'm very glad to see you! I heard there was a lady in the private room, and never dreamt I should be lucky enough to find an acquaintance!"

The waiting-maid, strange to say, was not in the least imposed upon by this *ruse;* and Renée detected a lurking smile on the said astute Elizabeth's mouth, as she bent over the fire to put on more coals.

"I'll bring up a second cup," she said, grinning again; "and will you have an extra tea-pot, or the tea set out on one table?" Then she looked out of the corner of her eyes at the handsome young soldier. She would hardly perhaps have been astonished had she seen the greeting that passed between this pair, the door being shut at last behind her. Huddersfield drew Renée towards him, and then holding her for a minute by both hands, he looked at her with his usual half-insolent expression of proprietorship.

"You are wonderful!" he said, smiling all the time that he spoke. "Every day you grow younger and lovelier, I really think. What you will end in at last, I don't know!"

And he put one arm round her slender neck, lifting her lips to meet his own.

"What a funny place for us to meet in, my dear child. It is like your romantic mind to have imagined it!"

"Well, I felt I *must* see you, Billy. Every day I think of you and long to know what you do. I don't suppose, though, you devote much spare time to meditating upon me?" She looked up at him half pitifully, with passionate eyes. For all answer he kissed her again.

"I only know that I am very happy in your company, my Renée. It has been quite fatal to me being thrown so much with you this last month. It don't give me a chance of forgetting, you see!"

His arm around her, he led her to a black horsehair-covered arm-chair and made her sit down. Then he seated himself on the elbow, and smoothed her dark wavy hair with his hand.

"What a pity, little Renée, that we can't stay on here, you and I, at the Barley Mow. It would be very pleasant, with no one to interfere with us in our isolation, wouldn't it?"

She laughed nervously, but he saw that she trembled from head to foot.

"Ah! yes, 'the world forgetting, by the

world forgot,' to use a trite quotation.
Which of us would tire of it first? Oh,
you; think of the 'good plain cooking,' and
the sour claret!"

"We would make long excursions all
over the country," continued Huddersfield,
as if he were telling a story to a child;
"we would have snug little dinners, and play
piquet afterwards. And you should read
aloud to me in the evenings while I smoked."

"What is the use of talking such utter
nonsense?"

"It amuses me, and it's a comfort,
stranded as I am between India and my
heiress, to think, if only for ten minutes,
of what life might be!"

Renée began to pour out tea from a huge
nickel tea-pot. This little meal in the
parlour at the Barley Mow seemed to her
excellent, and Huddersfield at any rate eat
enough to deprive himself of all possible
appetite for dinner.

The light began to wane a little, and the maid, still on the broad grin, looked in to know if "they'd like a gas-burner lit, or a pair o' candles?"

"What do you say; don't you think the dusk is nicer?"

Outside several carts and flys followed each other in quick succession past the inn door.

"You're quite gay here," said Huddersfield to the maid, who was removing the tea-things.

"Oh yes, sir, there's a Primrose League meeting a-going on, and a concert. Them there's the people coming home. They're from all parts."

Renée looked out at a substantial farmer and his wife, stopping at the inn door. They asked for beer, which was handed out to them, and held a few minutes' conversation with the landlord. Then their white horse jogged off again, and from a light that streamed from the Barley Mow across the road it was clear that the gas was alight now down-stairs.

"Elizabeth, come down to the bar!" called a strident voice from below. And the smiling attendant vanished.

"What time is your train, dear?" asked Huddersfield.

"Oh, I think about a quarter to seven. I shall be awfully late for dinner, but my father has been having his up-stairs lately, so it don't matter."

"Well, it is most good of you to have come all this long way. I hate your having to go back in the dark alone. But we have lots of time still. It's only a little after five."

A shut carriage, of rather greater pretensions than the former passing vehicles, drew up at the inn door. From it emerged a stout gentleman in a fur-lined coat, followed by a short lady disguised in mufflings and cloaks.

"They are coming in!" said Renée. "I only hope they won't show them up here."

Huddersfield crossed the room and opened the door. Voices were audible below, and one sounded very familiar to the two people in No. 14.

"We should be extremely glad if we could be accommodated with a private sitting-room? My wife has need of a little rest. She felt very faint at the meeting, and I thought it best not to wait there for refreshments. Mary, my dear, let me divest you of your outer wrap?"

"Thanks, dear Daniel. Tea is an excellent restorative, I always say. I am sure I shall feel quite myself again very soon."

"I suppose, sir," said the landlord in an admiring and subservient voice, "that you 'ad a splendid overflow meeting? Very sorry I was, sir, not to 'ear your speech, being a sharer of your views. I expect the 'all was uncommon 'ot, and your good lady would be upset? If you don't mind, sir, 'aving of your tea in company with a lady and gentleman up above just now, we can make you very comfortable in No. 14. A good fire, sir, and an arm-chair to rest yourself!"

"I am sure we shall not object to your other guests, shall we, my dear Mary?" answered Mr. Prosser obligingly. "I will help you to remove your outer Shetland veil, and your woollen spencer, and then we will go up-stairs. I am glad to find," and the Q.C. turned approvingly to the land-lord, "that you are a staunch supporter of the party."

"Ah, yes, sir, and my missis 'ave got the Primrose brooch."

"And a very pretty ornament it is—Mr. Mr.—I did not catch your name."

"For heaven's sake, Renée, let's get out of this," said Huddersfield. "Old Mary

Prosser will never cease chattering if she meets us together here."

"Where can we go? It is a horrible bore!"

The young man rang the bell, and Elizabeth appeared.

"Hi, you—girl," he said, taking out half a sovereign, "will you show this lady—*look sharp*—into another room? bed-room, or anything will do."

The maid thought that she had grasped the situation. Here were a young couple, as handsome a one as you could wish to see, going, no doubt, to elope; and perhaps the relations or friends in pursuit were below.

"You come along with me, miss, this way," she said to Renée. "I'll show you missis's own bed-room. She ain't there, and she's got a fire, having had the tic awful bad in her face."

Mrs. Gore quickly followed Elizabeth up another flight of uncarpeted stairs, and Mr.

and Lady Mary Prosser came slowly up to No. 14.

Huddersfield, meanwhile, wearing a perfectly calm and *nonchalant* air, stood with his back to the fire.

"Gracious, Prosser! Where are you from? How are you, Lady Mary? Oh, I believe you've bossed the show at the meeting, haven't you? Had a good audience?"

"Daniel was the principal speaker," answered Lady Mary, "if that is what you mean. Yes, he had a capital audience. I have always understood that the Hampshire labourer is not very intelligent, but he seemed, dear, did he not, to grasp your points? Daniel's voice carries so well too, Lord Huddersfield; and he touched a good deal upon agriculture, which of course came home to the people. He warned them to beware of agitators, he represented to them how really comfortable and prosperous they ought to be."

Mr. Prosser, looking in any case undeniably prosperous and smug himself, warmed his hands over the blaze.

"I hope we may have won some new recruits to the League," he remarked. "We are staying with an ardent supporter, Mr. Drinkwater, the other side of Widhurst. Where are you from, Huddersfield?"

"Aldershot. I stopped here to get my pony shod, and have had some excellent tea, meanwhile."

Lady Mary divested herself of a few more woollen garments, and with a fast-crimsoning nose, sat down close to the fireplace.

"A very tidy room this, Mary. Really quite a decent print of dear Lord Beaconsfield, and one or two of our favourite Landseers."

Mr. Prosser, who was in a benignant frame of mind, walked up and down the room, looking at the walls through his eyeglass. Huddersfield wondered how long Renée's enforced imprisonment would last. He exchanged glances with Elizabeth, when she brought in a smoking tray.

"I have ordered a couple of poached eggs, Mary. I feel I want a little sustaining after my speech! One must keep up the system, Huddersfield, more even when one does brain work than if one is in the habit of taking violent physical exercise. Shall I butter you a piece of toast, dearest? I think you look better already for the warmth of this pleasant room. I will order the brougham" (Mr. Prosser pronounced it *brawm*) "in half an hour. By that time we shall feel, I hope, thoroughly refreshed and rested."

Huddersfield looked at the clock. It was a good deal after six. He was immensely provoked at the unexpected end of his interview with Renée, and became very absent when Mr. Prosser, his mouth full of

buttered toast, began to expatiate on the
work done by the Primrose League in his
newly-adopted county of Shropshire.

"We have started a Prosser Habitation,
of which my dear wife is Dame President.
She is indefatigable in distributing leaflets."
Here the Q.C. helped himself to strawberry
jam. "By the way, Gore, that man whom
we met at Strathrowan, has written to ask
me if I can come and speak for him some
time or other. I must try to do so. Have
you seen anything of the Gores since our
pleasant Highland visit, Huddersfield?"

"Now and then. Yes, they are very
nice people."

Lady Mary's lips were pursed up as she
observed—"Hardly suited to one another
though, one would be afraid. He is so
thoroughly the rural squire; and she—well,
there is something very un-English about
her. I remember so well people comparing
her and Mrs. Hesseltine, as two beauties, at

a Queen's Ball. Léontine Hesseltine is, I think, *lovely*, and so thoroughly ladylike. Which do you admire most, Lord Huddersfield ? "

" They are so entirely different. Both beautiful, I am sure of that."

" Quite so, quite so," responded the Q.C. And his wife looked a little annoyed.

" Daniel never knows whether a woman is pretty or not," she said, naïvely.

The clock struck seven.

" Well, dear, shall I assist you into your furs ? We shall keep our kind Drinkwaters waiting for dinner if we linger on." And Mr. Prosser smiled down upon the empty dishes. A few more minutes and they were gone, and a light footstep sprang down the stairs.

" Am I in time for my train ? "

" Just—if you make a run for it. By Jove ! old Prosser is getting out again at the corner and coming back. Good Lord ! This is enough to madden a saint !"

"I think Lady Mary left a veil in your up-stairs room. Perhaps I had better go up myself to make sure?" said the Q.C.'s voice from below.

"No, sir, don't trouble; I'll run," shouted Elizabeth, and she shortly appeared breathless at the door of No. 14.

"The gentleman 'll be up in a second, sir, if you can't find that there veil!"

"Here it is—an old Shetland horror," said Renée.

"Elizabeth, you are a first-rate girl. Here's another half-sovereign for you."

There was a whistle from the station. Mrs. Gore stamped her foot on the floor.

"Come on," said Huddersfield, "the South-Western's always late. We must run like steam." And through the damp cold evening air he and she went swiftly, arriving panting just one minute before the train started.

"Good-night, good-night! It's been rather

a *fiasco*, this meeting. But still it's better than nothing!"

"Yes, ever so much better. Good-bye. Take care of yourself. And we must meet soon—somehow."

There was a jar of the wheels, and Huddersfield took his foot off the step, giving a last pressure to her hand. And he watched the white smoke and the sparks of fire from the engine till they vanished in the growing mist.

# CHAPTER IX.

"WELL, my dear old chap, I'm sure we're awfully pleased to welcome you and Mrs. Hesseltine here. Come to the fire and warm yourselves. Jos, old boy, say how do you do, nicely. Deuced cold for travelling, I'm afraid? Renée ought to have been down to see you, only she got damp going down to the village to look after poor old Aunt Isabella."

"How pretty your drawing-room is, Mr. Gore," said little Léo, who looked white and tired after her journey.

"All Renée's choosing. She understands

comfort, that girl does. We shall have a cup o' tea in here directly, and that'll warm you up a bit."

There was a rustle of draperies, and Mrs. Gore, as usual, simply but beautifully dressed, glided in. She kissed Léontine affectionately, and gave a very cordial hand-shake to Frank. And as she poured out tea, she devoted most of her conversation to the latter, for which she was hardly to be blamed, for Léontine leant wearily back in her chair, and scarcely answered any observation, excepting by monosyllables. She was certainly changed since her marriage a year ago, sweet and gentle as ever, but graver and more indifferent to her surround-ings. Once or twice Frank had held counsel with himself as to whether it would not be better to tell her honestly that he knew the cause of her sadness ; that he understood and forgave it, but that as they would inevitably have to live their lives together, it would be well to try and wear a more smiling countenance, at least in face of the world. But then on second thoughts he repelled the idea of this scheme, as being unlikely to mend matters much. Being of a sensitive, over-humble disposition, the sudden collapse of his hopes tried him cruelly ; and the result was an occasional coldness and impatience of manner towards his wife, of which he was almost unaware. And in Léontine's poor little wounded heart the tortures of jealousy festered and rankled, and she too underwent a change of bearing, growing as silent and chilly as he. There were moments of course in which this foolish pair of people were still as happy as it perhaps falls to the lot of ordinary mortals to be ; but one of them, at least, had started on their joint life expecting much more than this, and the other had begun to feel that she had acquired an undreamt-of joy, just as it seemed about to be torn from her grasp.

"I have only just returned from Surrey," observed Renée. "I came back two days ago with my small boy, for papa had an old cousin coming to stay with him. It is always pleasant to be settled at home for many reasons, though I miss the Surrey air. It is very damp and raw here."

"I suppose you were extremely quiet at your old home?"

"Extremely so. I always am. I don't think I came across an acquaintance the whole time, or only about once."

"I thought you said Huddersfield had been over to luncheon?" said Anthony.

"Oh yes, to be sure. I had forgotten him. He is very full of a plan for starting for India. It seems almost a pity, doesn't it, to give up his good staff appointment? Have some more tea-cake, Léo? You really eat nothing!"

"The railway often tries my head. If

you will allow me, I will go and rest a little now before dinner."

Frank sighed and threw himself back in his chair.

"Ah," he thought, "she cannot bear even to hear Huddersfield discussed. And how much tact Mrs. Gore showed in never mentioning him till that blundering old Anthony lugged his name in!" Then he said aloud—

"Yes, Léo, you had much better go and lie down. You mustn't have neuralgia when you are here. We want to show you all the beauties of the country."

"There's not much to see, Mrs. Hesseltine," interposed Anthony; "a bit of a ruin and a church or two, if you care for those sort of mouldy old things. We are not very well off for neighbours, but such as they are, they're awfully nice and friendly, don't you know. They come over in a cheery sort of way and take a bite with us, just alone.

Pettifer, that's my vicar, and his wife dine
here this evening, by the way. He's a good
sort, old Pettifer is; and Admiral Mullins
and his daughter, aren't they booked for to-
night, Renée?" Mr. Gore rubbed his hands
and looked very much pleased with the
world in general; while his wife escorted
Léontine to her room. On her return she
found Frank sitting alone, Anthony having
disappeared to interview a man with some
ferrets for sale.

"It is very pleasant to be here again,
Mrs. Gore."

"It is so good of you to say so; for I
know well how profoundly dull it is. I
wouldn't say so for worlds to my good Tony,
but it *is*, and the climate *is* so raw and
cold. Then he will—it is very dear and
hospitable of him—ask heavy neighbours to
dinner, and I can't stop him doing it. Old
Mullins is a fearful bore. Like most of the
people in the neighbourhood, he is deaf,

and he has a cough that does not change with times and seasons—it is permanent. He was in the White Sea and the China War, and I believe has lots of medals, but he never hears you if you do try to ask him questions."

"Well, I am really not easily bored. Besides, I shall perhaps have the luck to sit next to my hostess?"

"To be sure you will. There is the gong for dressing."

Léontine, in pale green velvet, came into the drawing-room punctually at eight, to find the Pettifers and the Admiral and his daughter already there; and Anthony, who had triumphantly put on a new scarlet hunting-coat, and forgotten to take the paper off the hinder buttons, gave her his arm. On her other side sat the nautical hero; and in accordance with her husband's previous advice, she asked him about his past career, speaking as loudly she could—

"You were in the White Sea operations against the Russians, were you not?" The Admiral stared at her, coughed and choked, and put his hand up to his ear.

"What does she say?" he asked of his daughter, a thin and depressed old maid who sat facing him.

"She says, papa—"

"May I ask you to stop a moment?" said Anthony, also very loudly, as if the whole world were deaf, "Mr. Pettifer is about to say grace."

The Admiral, with his shoulder turned away from Mrs. Hesseltine, melted a pill in his soup, and began to swallow it in large gulps. Léontine, still blushing, and thinking it was no use pursuing the subject of the Russian wars, entered into conversation with Anthony, who was in high spirits.

"You must have a talk with Pettifer about schools, if you're interested in that sort of thing, Mrs. Hesseltine. He has started a

musical drill, which is ripping. Oh, by
the way, what an ass I am! I forgot to tell
the Crabston band to come and play to us
to-night while we're eating."

"The band's outside, sir," said the butler,
in a loud stage whisper. "But the young
man from opposite the King's Arms has
put his elbow through the big drum, sir."

"Never mind, they can play without it,
I suppose. Tell 'em to start with 'It's a
fine hunting day.'"

There was a deafening cough from Admiral
Mullins, a large forked bone from one of
Anthony's favourite pike having stuck cross-
ways in his throat. His host promptly rose
and thumped him on the back; and with
tears running down his face, the Admiral was
able soon afterwards to resume his dinner.

Léontine, who was afraid of appearing
discourteous, made one more effort to address
him—

"I understand you were in the China war?"

After repeating this observation three times, her neighbour appeared to grasp her meaning.

"I should think I *was!* I've got a couple of bullets in me still, don't yer know that? One here," and he thumped his chest, "and another lower down. Feel 'em in this weather." And another paroxysm of coughing shook his weather-beaten frame, bullets and all.

The Crabston band, playing noisily in the hall, obviated all further necessity for conversation. Anthony ordered "A Life on the Ocean Wave," in compliment to his distinguished guest; and Mrs. Pettifer begged for the "Lost Chord." In the rendering of the latter well-known piece, however, many more chords than one appeared to be absent on this occasion.

After dinner, Léo could not but admire Mrs. Gore's courtesy to her guests. She listened patiently to Miss Mullins's account of her recent bitter warfare with the cook, whom the Admiral had found prostrate under the table on the afternoon of his last dinner-party ; and to Mrs. Pettifer's explanation of which of the nine young Pettifers had had the measles lightly, and which of them with varied complications.

When the men came out of the dining-room, Frank Hesseltine made his way across the room to where his hostess was sitting.

"The old sea-dog has done himself pretty well," he said with a smile ; "I fear his cough isn't likely to be better after some brown sherry, a bottle of old *Dagonet*, and several glasses of Tony's best crusted."

Admiral Mullins, walking as if a heavy gale were blowing, his gray hair standing on end, and his face very crimson, proposed a rubber.

"I sha'n't be up to my usual form," he explained. "The damp weather touches me up. I can feel the bullets. They

twinge a bit. It's no use, Jane, your
cutting in," (a violent fit of coughing here
interrupted him), "you generally revoke,
and I can't drive into your stupid head
how to ask for trumps."

Mr. Pettifer mildly suggested that *he*
would take a hand, if Mr. Gore wished it ;
so together with Anthony, Admiral Mullins,
and Léoutine, he sat down at the card-
table. When he found that his partner
was to be the irascible Admiral, he shook
in his laced boots, and devoutly wished that
he had remained looking at the photograph
books.

"Come on, come on, Mr. Pethybridge ;
don't take twenty minutes to deal. Ha !"
and the nautical hero's eyes glared when
he discovered that a pitiful little two of
spades was his only trump. The game
went on. "Mind what you're about !"
roared Admiral Mullins ; "you don't seem
to understand the *rudiments* of whist !

I'm dashed if I ever saw such play as that! Good Lord, Mr. Pethybridge; can't you keep your eye open to see what Gore's just put down! I'll be hanged if I ever ask a parson to play whist again, I'm—"

Mr. Pettifer was trembling, but preserved his dignity and a certain amount of composure.

"I was not aware that you *did* ask me, Admiral Mullins. I have been in the habit of taking a hand here at Crabston, but I have *not* been accustomed to be spoken to in such language!"

And almost alarmed at his own boldness, Mr. Pettifer glanced across the room at his wife.

"Only my chaff; goodness me!" said the Admiral, who had just discovered three honours in his hand. "You mustn't mind a man's speaking his mind out a bit." (A loud fit of coughing.) "You're not doing much in the way of tricks, hay, Gore?

Ha, ha! You didn't expect that king, hay?"

"I think," observed Mr. Pettifer, meekly yet firmly, "you trumped clubs just now, Admiral Mullins. Of course we didn't expect to see the King of Clubs after that! It's to my own loss, but one must be honest at cards, as at all things!"

Anthony kicked Mr. Pettifer with his large foot.

"You'd better not irritate the Admiral, especially after dinner!" he said in a loud whisper.

But it was too late. Rear-Admiral Mullins, of the Retired List, now displayed such an extraordinary ebullition of temper, that Anthony thought it prudent to tell a white lie, and contradict his vicar.

"I fear that I cannot play, Mr. Gore, if we are not to be conscientious!" said the latter firmly.

"Conscience?" shouted the Admiral.

" Your conscience be hanged! What conscience have *you* got to sit down to whist
with a man who has played with all the
swells in England for the last twenty years!
You don't seem to know a club from a
spade! The game had been ours but for
your confounded bad management. You
won't see me sit down with any more of
these pettifogging, shuffling—"

"Never mind, Admiral," said Anthony,
good-humouredly. " Let's have this rubber
out, and then change partners."

" Look at old Mullins!" said Hesseltine
to his hostess. " He's dropped half his
cards on the floor. I pity his daughter.
She must have a bad time when the
weather's damp, and he feels the bullets."

Léontine had found time, in spite of
playing a fairly good game herself, and of
listening astonished to the fight between
her adversaries, to note that her husband
and Mrs. Gore seemed to be much amused

with one another. They were having their talk to themselves, for Mrs. Pettifer and Miss Mullins had embarked on the subject of Work Guilds, which seemed likely to keep their thoughts and tongues occupied for a long time to come. Léo felt dreadfully tired, and bored beyond expression; still, as she really liked the kind Anthony, she would not for worlds have shown him that she was not entertained by the game; and as he himself thoroughly enjoyed his rubber, it was quite pleasant to watch his face.

"Well, we'll have a second go, won't we?" said the squire. "What do you say, Admiral? It isn't late."

"I think if you will dispense with *me*, I should be grateful," murmured Mr. Pettifer.

Léontine was now paying the Admiral eighteen shillings, the last two games having recouped him, and he was chuckling with satisfaction.

" No thanks to you, Mr. Pethybridge !
*You* played a doosid odd kind of whist !
But all's well that ends well.   Mrs. Hesseltine, shall you and I be partners this
time ?   You've got a memory, I can see
that ; *you* won't make stoopid blunders,
hay ? "

Poor Léo was trying to suppress a yawn
behind her little hand.

" Won't some of you others come instead
of me ?   Frank, you are very good at
whist."

Her husband saw how pale she looked,
and rose from his chair.

" You had better go and get a good sleep,
Léo.   Just slip away," he said kindly,
coming towards her.   She looked up at him
with a half-grateful, half-sad expression.

" Thanks, Frank ; I do feel rather done
up and seedy to-night."

" I'll come and play," said Mrs. Gore,
advancing towards the table.   " What do

you say, Mr. Hesseltine, to you and I, against Tony and the Admiral ? "

" By all means. What shall we play, Anthony, shillings and half-crowns ? "

"That's it. I am so sorry you're done up, Mrs. Hesseltine ; but you'll find Crabston air famous for making you sleep. I feel in the mornings that I must turn over and have another snooze before I can harden my heart to kick the clothes off."

In spite of the properties of the far-famed Crabston air, Léontine, tired as she was, tossed sleeplessly about on her bed. She pictured Frank and Renée smiling at each other across the green table, the shaded candles casting a glow on her radiant face ; the Admiral doubtless swearing at his host, while Tony remained silent and good-humoured throughout.

" *I* never saw such cards ! What in Heaven's name can a man do with a hand like this ? It's just my cursed luck " (a fit of coughing). " Gore, you didn't twig that I asked for trumps ! Where, may I ask you, were your eyes ? I thought you knew the rules of the game ! I call that infernally stoopid of you ! P'r'aps you'd just send for a whiskey-and-soda for me ? My cough's uncommon bad to-night. Lord bless me ! you've gone and wasted your *best* card !"

The Admiral's eyes shone like green glass marbles, and he extended a trembling hand towards the middle of the table. And meanwhile, his daughter, who was accustomed to his ways, went on calmly discussing calico chemises and flannel petticoats with Mrs. [Pettifer. The rubber was over at last, the Admiral given another whiskey-and-soda, and wrapped in a plaid shawl, and a head-dress like that of an Arctic explorer. He expressed himself as delighted with his evening, and asked the Gores to come and dine with him as often as they liked, and to "bring that doosid good-looking woman with fair hair, Mrs. What-d'ye-call-her ; and old Pethybridge, and any one else you wish."

Mrs. Pettifer changed her lace cap for a shady hat, drew on her galoshes and water-proof cloak, and started homewards with her vicar, who had evidently not enjoyed himself so much as the Admiral had done.

"Did it strike you, dear," she said, as they passed through the park gates, "that that gentleman with the dark beard, Mr. Hesseltine, I mean, was rather too attentive to Mrs. Gore ? Of course I don't mean anything in the least *wrong*, but I am not used to the ways of people like that. She isn't my style, you know, dear."

"*I* think her a very nice agreeable person. But you women are all alike, my love ; you imagine things that no man would. Take care, you are losing a galosh. I do wish that Admiral Mullins would learn to control himself. To me it is positively painful to see an old man give way to evil tempers in that manner. His language was shocking."

The following morning, Renée, who was reading her letters at breakfast, exclaimed—

" I wonder if it would bore you dreadfully, Léo, to go to-morrow to a little dance —not a regular ball—at the Wheldales' ? Should you hate it ? we needn't stop late."

" Oh, no, I shall be very glad to go."

" It's a pretty house, and everything is sure to be well done. Tony, you can air your new red coat, my dear boy."

" There's a moon too, which is a good job," said Anthony cheerfully. " And the chestnut mare's sound again now, that's a piece of luck, too."

It was about half-past ten when the Gores' carriage, the old-fashioned heavy green landau, drew up at Lord Wheldale's front door. The hostess greeted them most

warmly; for two such beautiful women as
Renée and Mrs. Hesseltine are not often
seen among a group of fifty people in the
country. Mrs. Gore was in rose-colour,
with her diamond crown glittering on her
head. The faithful Tony, as he gazed at
it and her, did not once sigh as he thought
of his put-off farm-improvements, and the
empty stalls in his stable; he looked as
happy as his wife, if less brilliant.

There was a suppressed murmur of admiration when Léontine followed Renée into
the well-lighted room. Her long train of
sky-blue velvet swept the polished boards,
the fit of her dress was miraculous, so the
ladies one and all declared; and the mass
of silver embroidery on the skirt was greatly
admired by a row of whispering *ingénues*.
Nothing could have been lovelier than the
soft clusters of fair hair on her little head,
and her tiara of diamonds and turquoises,
one of Frank's numerous presents, was even

prettier than Renée's crown. There was
one tall man standing in the embrasure of
a door who started visibly at the sight of
this fairy-like apparition in blue and silver.

"Who is that wonderfully pretty woman
with flaxen hair?" asked his partner, who
happened to be one of his host's daughters.

"She's a Mrs. Hesseltine, and is a
German by birth; Countess Léontine Wartburg her name was before she married."

"Well, she *is* too sweet! I admire her
ever so much more than Mrs. Gore; don't
you?"

"Shall we have another turn, Lady
Katie? I think we ought to keep it up,
as there are not very many of us to
dance."

The valse over, Lord Huddersfield, having
left Lady Katie on a sofa, crossed the room
to where Lord Wheldale was talking to
Mrs. Hesseltine. He waited for a few
minutes, until his host had bustled off again,

and then he asked her anxiously if her arm was entirely well, and if she felt quite strong now, and many other questions.

"Come and have a dance," he said ; and presently, to the swinging cadences of a German air, the two floated round the room, he valsing so well that motion seemed a rest instead of a fatigue. "Let us go and see how pretty they have made the conservatory."

Then, as she hesitated, he added—

"I am not going to say *one* word of which you would disapprove. I *swear* it."

She laid her hand on his arm, and crossing the ball-room, they passed through the yellow drawing-room, in which a few older people, including Admiral Mullins, were playing whist, and entered the high conservatory lighted with rose-shaded electric lamps.

Huddersfield led the way to a sofa at one end, and they sat down.

"I want," he said, abruptly, "to ask

your advice. Shall I marry Miss MacGwire-Jones or not ? "

" Is she the heiress I have heard of ? "

" She is ; and I really don't dislike her. You know, Mrs. Hesseltine, what my history has been, more or less,—no, don't turn away ; I *swear* I will not say a word to hurt you. I fear, though, that I am worse even than you think. I have got into a kind of entanglement now that is harder than most of the sort to get out of. I don't wish to exculpate myself. I have behaved infernally badly, and I may do, have perhaps done, fatal harm. If my marriage would make it easier to get out of this scrape, should I marry ? "

He looked at her pure and beautiful face very earnestly, and sighed ; thinking, perhaps, of the fatal " No more, Too late, Farewell," the motto of so many lives.

" What do you advise, Countess Léo ? "

he said again, speaking very low. "Help me—I cannot help myself."

Léontine was tender-hearted, and she had once liked this man more than a little. She was touched now at his confidence, at his desire for her counsel, at the gentle submissiveness of his manner. And the tears actually glittered in her deep violet eyes as she listened to him.

"If, as you say, you like this girl, and your marriage with her might be the beginning of a different kind of life to you, perhaps it would be a good step. I always feel, though, that it is dangerous to give advice on these sort of occasions. How little the wisest among us can judge as to the happiness or disaster of marriages! Lord Huddersfield, you must know best yourself. But do, *do* in any case try to get honourably out of this new entanglement, whatever it may be!"

Just then, Frank Hesseltine, who was

waiting till Mrs. Gore should have finished a quadrille, and be ready to dance with him, strolled into the conservatory by the opposite door from which Léo and her partner had entered. He started, and turned a little pale when he saw his wife absorbed in conversation with Huddersfield. Hesseltine observed the tears shining in her eyes, giving them a greater brilliancy, the earnestness of her manner as she spoke to the man sitting beside her, and the quiet intentness of his attitude as he listened. Sick at heart, he clenched his hands together, and went slowly out by the door through which he had come. When he approached Mrs. Gore she noticed that something had occurred to distress him, and almost instantly she divined what it was. Her manner became more gentle and sympathetic than ever, and Frank, even in his utter gloom, found her thrilling voice soothing, and was grateful to her for her

efforts to divert his thoughts. He danced
twice with her, a fact that did not pass
unobserved by Léo, and took her in to
supper. Renée, although she smiled almost
as much as usual, was undergoing a pain
no less bitter than that of those other two.
She had waited now for two hours or more,
and there was no sign that Huddersfield
meant even to address a word to her. He
had bowed courteously, but was obviously
avoiding her. Once she was close to his elbow
while a dance was going on, and she had
resolved to speak to him; but he, perhaps
guessing her intention, had started off again
with his partner, and when they had paused
again, panting a little after their exertion, it
was at the furthest end of the large ball-
room. Mrs. Gore was obliged to make violent
efforts to screw herself up to the pitch of
listening to, and answering, her partner,
a fat and heated young squire, in a scarlet
coat. He remarked afterwards to a friend,

that he was sure "Mrs. Gore had a fiendish temper; he spotted that by her face when her mouth was shut."

Léontine's soft pink colour had died away, and the tired look which her face so often wore now was on her eyes and brow. She tried to speak to Frank as she left the supper-room.

"Don't you think, Frank, we might be going soon?"

"Whenever you and Mrs. Gore choose." He spoke so curtly that she was startled.

"It has been a very pretty dance, hasn't it, Frank?"

"I suppose it has."

Her husband turned away, and began talking about hunting with two other men. Léontine felt suddenly cold and faint. Why was he so angry? Then she saw that Mrs. Gore was sitting in a corner of the ball-room, talking to a very good-looking partner, with a waxed moustache.

Ah! Frank was vexed, perhaps, that Mrs. Gore should be engrossed with any one but himself.

"Where shall I take you?" said Léo's partner, as they wandered rather aimlessly among the dancers.

"Oh, I don't know. Anywhere. Don't let me keep you. I'll sit here on this seat, and look at the people."

And growing giddy, she watched a medley of figures, in white and scarlet and blue, with long and short legs, scarlet and pale faces, energetic men and flabby women, limp boys and buxom girls, whirling round and round, and wondered how on earth they could feel amused. Lord Huddersfield passed her alone.

"You look awfully tired, Mrs. Hesseltine. May I call the carriage?"

"You must ask Mrs. Gore."

At that moment Renée and Frank came through a doorway together. Lord Huddersfield, with a *sang-froid* that did him in one sense credit, cruel though it was, advanced towards Mrs. Gore.

"Mrs. Hesseltine looks tired," he said. "Can I be of any use in getting the carriage?"

She shot a curious defiant glance at him; a look that was anything but agreeable.

"Thanks; my husband will see about it."

And Hesseltine, his heart aching, thought what a loyal friend Mrs. Gore was. She knew of his trouble, of that he felt sure, and therefore she was angry with Lord Huddersfield, to the point of being almost rude to him.

"We'll find Tony," said Renée. "I am awfully sorry dear Léo is tired. Let's see if that lazy old boy of mine is among the whist-players. He can't dance."

In the yellow drawing-room Anthony was discovered, likewise Admiral Mullins, who had lost two rubbers, and was standing by a whist-table, gesticulating in a sort of blind fury.

"I'll tell you what it is," he shouted, "it's doosid poor fun to play whist anywhere out of one's club. The game was ours, Milligan, upon my soul it was, and there ain't any use your denying it. You lost five tricks in one game by your devilish stoopid play. It's sickening. I'm a poorer man by four pun' ten than I was when I came into this room!"

Anthony expressed his willingness to get the carriage at once.

"It's been a jolly evening, hasn't it?" he said. "All the right people, and a thundering good feed. Drinks excellent, as usual, here. I've won a bit too, Renée, though you do crab my play. All right, old girl, I'm off. You go and say goodnight to her ladyship."

Lord Huddersfield and a few other young men staying in the house came out into

the hall to see the departures. He gave
his arm to Léontine, who was standing
silently under a lamp, wrapped in a long
cloak of silver brocade. As he put her
into the carriage he whispered—

"I am going to take your advice. And,"
he added, in so low a tone that she could
not hear him, "perhaps I have begun
to-night."

The carriage lumbered along over the
road in the cold early morning. Léo's eyes
were shut, so that she was unaware of the
peculiar gaze that Mrs. Gore fixed upon her
from time to time.

"There is nothing," thought that last-
named lady, "that I would not do to injure
her! It is she, and she alone, who wrecks
my life. He would care for me—he was
beginning to be so different—and then she
comes between us again. No, Léo, don't
think I don't know what's passing in your
mind. *You* are not in love with him;

but you have stolen his heart from me,
and I will make you suffer where your heart
*is* touched, just as you have tortured me."

"Home at last!" cried Anthony. "No
place like home after all. You must wake
up, Frank, old chap. Have a basin of hot
soup and a sandwich before you turn in!
Well, I must say we've had a first-class
evening! I hope all you three enjoyed
yourselves?"

And without waiting for an answer, Mr.
Gore took a header over the carriage foot-
warmer, landed on the steps, and proceeded
to help the ladies to descend.

# CHAPTER X.

" WELL, I must say you all three look uncommonly cheap this morning! Any one can see you've been up all night. Mrs. Hesseltine, you should have had a bit of food in your room. And it's awfully cold! Look at it, trying to snow ; the ground 'll be all wet and sloshy."

Anthony Gore piled up his plate with kidneys and bacon, and went on talking with his mouth full.

" Well, you don't seem very cheerful, any of you. Very sorry you have to go to-morrow, old chap. I must say I thought it a ripping dance last night. Old Wheldale always does you well, that I will say. None of your gooseberry at thirty shillings, but real good drinks. I say, Renée, tomorrow's Saturday, and we've got, haven't we, the tea in the village coming off? Wish you could have stayed over it, Mrs. Hesseltine. Tea for the Sunday School children and a few others, and a concert afterwards, for the older people."

"I wish we could, but Frank thought we ought to be back at Ledsham."

Léontine's voice did not express any very deep regret. She was opening her letters, and a sudden smile of pleasure came over her face, often so sad now, as she recognized the handwriting on one of them.

"Here's a letter from Louise Valendar, Frank," she said, tearing it open. "Oh! *how* nice, she's in London now! But I am afraid her aunt must be very ill, for her to have come over suddenly like this. Frank, I wonder, would you very much mind my going straight to London to see her, instead of returning to Ledsham? I could join you in a few days."

"Certainly, dear, go if you like."

Renée glanced up at Frank. He looked pale and drawn, and so sad, that it was odd that even that very dense Anthony did not notice it. But Hesseltine made efforts to shake off his melancholy, and began to talk about the ball.

"There was rather an absence of beauty, wasn't there, last night? Lady Katie Sutton is pretty, but I hardly saw any one else to admire."

"Poor Miss Mullins didn't dance much," said Anthony, speaking indistinctly with his mouth full of tea-cake. "I took her for a turn, but she was a dead weight in the polka. I'm a poor dancer, and she always gets giddy. I wonder, did any one ask

Huddersfield about his heiress? I meant to, but it went out of my head."

Léontine blushed, and Frank answered a little impatiently—

"It wouldn't have shown much tact if you had."

"Didn't think of that, Frank. P'r'aps you're right. If he hasn't settled, he wouldn't like to be bothered. Gracious, look at the flakes of snow now, big as my thumb! What are you ladies going to do?"

"Toast ourselves over the fire," answered Renée. "I don't want to catch cold, Tony, before your hilarious village tea to-morrow."

She rose, and Anthony began scraping up the crumbs, and cutting up bits of fat for the birds, in which occupation he received valuable assistance from Jos, who had just entered the room.

"It's time your curls were cut, old man," said his uncle, shaking the boy's golden locks. They were great friends, these two, and were very happy together now as they went round collecting the scraps, and speculating as to which birds would come first. Then Anthony flung open the window, and a cold damp current of air rushed in. They stood watching.

"There's the nuthatch!" said the child, in a tone of the keenest delight, squeezing his uncle's arm. "What a sweet he is! And the same dear puffy old blackbird who was here yesterday. The robins are driving the poor darling little chaffinch away!" All this was said in a half whisper, Jos quivering with excitement the while.

Renée had meanwhile ordered the dinner, interviewed her maid on the subject of a new gown, and gone up-stairs to her own room. She carefully bolted the door, and sat down at her writing-table, with a curious expression on her face. Evidently she had some important work on hand, for during the next ten minutes or so she sat

almost motionless, lost in thought, an elbow
on the table, her chin resting on one palm.
Outside the landscape seemed singularly
silent and cheerless. The rather stunted
trees in Crabston Park looked like small
skeletons against a leaden sky. Flakes of
snow, some of them very large, were floating noiselessly down, many of them melting
as soon as they touched the sodden earth.
Most of the birds had gone round to the
windows where Anthony and Jos were
standing, so the air seemed lifeless. Just
across the park was the broad pond which
Tony dignified by the name of the lake, the
home of his favourite pike. The road leading to the village was deserted, except for
the figure of one bent old woman carrying
a faggot on her back.

Within, the room was bright enough. A
fire roared up the chimney, pleasantly reflected in the shining grate. A nosegay or
two of hot-house flowers shed a delicious

perfume over the blue and white chintz
hangings, and the pale blue plush *portières*
that screened the doors. On the numberless little tables and shelves, mostly white
like the doors and chimney-piece, were
books and photographs, and the dressing-
table positively blazed with a multitude of
silver boxes and brushes of all sizes.

Presently Renée opened her blotting-
book, also of silver, and took out a little
note, in a curious cramped handwriting. It
might, so far as the characters went, have
easily been the letter of a rather under-
educated school-boy of fourteen. The
signature was Léontine Hesseltine's, and
she wrote to thank Mr. and Mrs. Gore for
their invitation to Crabston, mentioning the
day on which they hoped to accept it. A
curious smile played over Renée's face for
a few moments. Then she actually laughed
aloud, a disagreeable laugh, although it was
neither harsh nor noisy.

She took a sheet of writing-paper from her envelope box, bearing the stamp of Crabston Hall at the top.

"It is not such a very easy task," she said to herself. "A vulgar conventional love-letter would certainly not do. No, it must be such a one as an honourable man, and one too proud to show his feelings, will never show the writer or make a subject of reproach. He must keep it to himself, and yet it must separate them entirely. It must be a letter that will ruin the happiness of her married life for ever. That happiness is tottering, I think, now on its foundations, and this must make it topple over into ruins. But it isn't an easy task. And then, there is always the off chance that if Mr. Hesseltine finds the letter he will have scruples about opening it. Ah, but I think I can get over that difficulty."

She paused again. "If, after all, he should accuse her of having written it?

No, he won't do that, if I write in the way
that I wish to do.   It will break his heart,
poor man ; but that is the most effectual
way of breaking hers."

Renée Gore rose up for a few moments,
and began walking up and down the room,
her hands clenched, her lips tightly set.
She was mentally reviewing the events of
the previous night. She saw the little
figure in blue and silver, arm-in-arm with
Lord Huddersfield ; his eyes bent upon Léo
with an expression that they never wore
when they gazed at her, Renée ; she suffered
over again the agony of waiting for him to
come and speak to her, the deferred hope,
the sickness and rage at her heart.   Then
her thoughts strayed back to her own meetings with her lover—was it only a few weeks
ago ?   And she hesitated no longer, but sat
down at her writing-table once more.

For two hours she wrote and re-wrote her
letter, tearing it up many times, and at last,

with the same cruel light in her eyes that
they had worn almost ever since she came
into her room, she finished and folded it.
Then she wrote one or two other letters
of no great importance, and went down,
with the three, into the drawing-room, where
Léo was sitting alone over the fire reading
*Maud.*

She stayed on for a few minutes, discussing Tennyson's poetry with Mrs. Hesseltine,
and went back to her room. As she passed
the window she noticed that a handkerchief
was lying on the floor. It was trimmed
with lace, and the name Léontine was
embroidered in one corner. Mrs. Gore
stooped down and put the handkerchief in
her pocket. Léo was sitting with her back
to her hostess, a large screen protecting
her from view. So she, of course, noticed
nothing; and Mrs. Gore, smiling to herself,
went up-stairs, singing on her way.

Towards three o'clock the snow abated

a little, and a dilapidated shut carriage drove up to the front door, just as Anthony and his guests were finishing luncheon.

"Rum day for a visitor!" exclaimed Tony. "Cold and beastly to turn out. But it's rather nice to have some one to come and cheer us up a bit."

"I don't think most of your neighbours would be likely to do that," his wife made answer with some asperity. "Oh, Tony, I wish I'd said 'not at home.' There's the Admiral's voice in the hall. What a horrible nuisance!"

"Poor old boy! He hasn't got much to do at his own house. He was very much smitten with you, Mrs. Hesseltine! That's why he honours us with a visit. I'll ask him to have a cup of coffee."

Mr. Gore went out into the hall, where the Admiral was divesting himself of his woollen shawl and muffetees.

"It's doosid dull at home, Gore," he said.

" Jane's laid up with a headache, over-eaten herself, I tell her, at that disgusting dance last night. So I thought I'd come over and look you up."

" *We* all thought it a capital ball," said the squire, taking the Admiral's plaid. "Sorry you were bored. Come and have some coffee. The weather won't get warmer till all the snow's down."

"Capital ball!" shouted the Admiral. "Well, I must say you're easily pleased. But you didn't play whist with three of the biggest asses in England, as I did. And the supper! Lord bless me! What d'ye think I got? A leg of pheasant, chuck-full o' shot. Then one of your nasty made-up things, all jelly and beastliness, of different colours. Never know what you're swallowing." And Admiral Mullins's cough here became very severe, but he resumed the subject. " I've upset myself for a week with that nasty food. I took a couple of liver pills the first thing this morning, and Jane cut me off my feed. Is luncheon over? For I might just have a mouthful now while you're about it."

The Admiral's brow grew a little smoother when Mrs. Hesseltine came up, and greeted him with her charming smile. He complimented her on her appearance on the preceding evening.

"Wished myself a young feller again, when I saw you!" he was kind enough to remark, and Léontine laughed.

"You never asked me to dance, after all, though, Admiral Mullins!"

"My dear, I wouldn't have the face to! Not but what I can move about as well, or better, than some of those grinning, clumsy young jackasses who go about treading on one's corns. Old Wheldale made a fool of himself, I thought, too, hopping about like a pea on a drum. Why, he has the gout worse than I have."

The Admiral sat down at the luncheon table, and the ladies left him to Anthony's care.

Mrs. Gore was decidedly very absent this afternoon ; but this fact made but little difference to Léo, who was thankful not to be obliged to talk to her. All day Frank had been silent too and depressed, and took little or no notice of his wife, thereby wounding her deeply. Mrs. Gore was perfectly well aware that he was unhappy, and forbore to vex him with questions or idle conversation. Towards evening she found him alone in the drawing-room, Léo having gone up-stairs.

" I am very sorry Léontine is going off to London, Mr. Hesseltine, to-morrow. But won't *you* stay on a day or two with us ? You'll be very dull all alone at Ledsham."

Frank hesitated. Perhaps it would be better, he thought, to stay on with his old friend Anthony, and the latter's lovely wife, than to wander about in solitude in the great rooms at the Towers.

"Well, I think I might manage to stop till Tuesday," he answered. "It's too nice of you to wish to keep me. I will make myself useful, and pour out tea for the people of Crabston to-morrow evening, if I'm wanted."

"We won't inflict that upon you. But it will be delightful if you stay."

When Frank went up-stairs to dress, he casually announced to his wife that he was remaining on a day or two longer at Crabston. In the dim light he did not see how very pale she had become.

"Then *I* may as well remain longer in London," she merely answered, shortly.

"As you choose. I mean to return home Tuesday."

Léontine made a violent effort to gulp down her tears, and answer, with some semblance of cheerfulness—

" All right, Frank; then I shall like to go home too that day."

He did not answer, and when he had left the room, she found that it was no use to try and keep back those tears any more.

# CHAPTER XI.

A COLD sleet was falling, and leaving little wet patches on the stone steps of Crabston Hall, as Léontine Hesseltine, wrapped in furs, came slowly down them. Her face was pale and her eyelids would have been seen to be suspiciously red, had they not been hidden by a thick veil. Her husband and Anthony followed her to the door of the shabby green landau, and Renée watched her departure from her drawing-room window. Léo had hoped that Frank would, at the last moment, offer to accom-

pany her to the station, but he had made
no suggestion of the kind; and only Mr.
Anthony Gore was profuse in his regrets at
being obliged to stay at home to interview
an ironmonger, the kitchen boiler having
recently begun to leak.

Frank's face was very sad as he watched
the heavy carriage slowly lumbering away
down the park. He appeared to take no
note of the falling sleet, which left cold
drops on his hair and beard. For five
minutes or more he remained on the steps,
hearing Anthony arguing at the top of his
voice in the offices, and apparently losing
his temper with both cook and tradesman.
Then he re-entered the house with an aching
heart. It was torture to him to feel that
he had parted coldly from his wife; even
now he was reproaching himself bitterly for
having allowed her to go away alone; and
then, almost simultaneously, he recalled the
scene at the Wheldales' dance—Hudders-

field bending over Léo's tearful little face—
the quivering of her lip, the passionate
earnestness of—what was the use of dis-
guising the facts ?—her lover's gaze. Just
for a moment, standing alone in the hall,
he covered his face with his hands, as if to
shut out that memory. He thought he
would go into the library, find an absorbing
book, if possible, and read it in the smoking-
room. As he passed the drawing-room door
he noticed a lace-trimmed handkerchief on
the mat. He stooped to pick it up, and
found that a blank envelope, evidently
drawn out of the pocket at the same time,
was beneath it. Yes, it was Léo's handkerchief, with her monogram embroidered at
the corner. The scent of the perfume
which she always used seemed to give him
a sudden stab of pain, and an acute sense of
her presence. Hesseltine turned it over.
He carried the letter and the flimsy little
handkerchief up-stairs into his room, shut

the window, through which a few snow-
flakes were floating in, and sat down by the
fire.

" I had better see what this is," he said,
" and if it is worth forwarding." And then
he began to read. The first words seemed to
burn themselves into his brain, to be rapped
out in a sort of measured cadence. Yet,
even then, he hardly understood their
meaning ; rather they left only a chill
sensation of despair within him. Two
deep lines, furrows almost, became marked
across his forehead, and his lips moved with
a nervous impulse that he could not control.
His hands felt so stiff and frozen that he
could hardly turn the page. When he had
read the letter through to the very end, he
re-read it, more than once, dwelling long
upon each sentence, sparing himself no
pang. His face showed no anger, rather
the blankness of an utter, a hopeless despair,
a gnawing grief that cannot know healing,

to which the solace of tears and human sympathy are denied.

This was what he had read, a letter with no formal beginning, and signed, "For the last time—Léo." Those words echoed in his brain with wearisome iteration.

"Unless we should meet, just once more, in London, this is good-bye for ever. We know, both of us, bitter as the knowledge is, blindly cruel as is Fate, that it is for the best. We told each other so, Bill (for the last time I write this word, *your* dear name), we agreed that we would help one another in the path of duty, that we would do our utmost to forget, not to darken the lives of those about us. Had you and I been allowed to belong to one another—oh! is it only two years ago?—I think life would have been paradise; but such happiness might have hindered us in other ways. We should have been too much absorbed in it, to the exclusion of what is still better.

With all my soul I do believe this also,
that in the future there may be joy of a
different kind, calmer and on a lower level,
but still genuine, for us both, if we try hard
to be good.

"I have married a man who has all my
esteem, and a measure of affection too,
which is, in its way, very real. I will try
to make him happy, Billy, honestly and
conscientiously, so you and I must not
meet. I will never ask you to come to my
house, never beg you to write to me or to
talk to me. I will devote myself hence-
forth to poor dear Frank, who is much too
kind to me. I don't feel as if I can write
more now. I am going to be in Carlton
Gardens for a few days, but I would rather
you did not call—I cannot see you alone,
never again. I hope and pray that you
may be happy in all your future. For the
last time—Léo."

Frank Hesseltine certainly did not know

if he sat on by the flickering logs for hours
or for minutes only. He seemed to have
lost all count of time. And ever and anon,
in the midst of his dumb anguish, old
sorrows and doubts revived, old pains were
born anew. He thought of Charles, of his
undying affection for him, of the trust which
this friend had confided to him, and which
it had been his deepest joy to fulfil, of the
downfall of all his hopes, the sickening
blank which was alone left, in lieu of light
and love. But all this time he had no
thought of reproach for the woman who had
brought him to this misery. It was not her
fault, poor child, if she could not care for
him, saddened and aged as he was even
when he had married her. He had asked
for too much, he had dreamed a foolish,
mad dream, and now was the time for its
forgetting. They must live their lives
together, he and she, for ten, twenty, thirty
years—pray God the end might come sooner

at least to him—always apart, yet wearing
smiling faces before the world. He must
help, not hinder her, in her self-imposed
task. And this could only be done by
ignoring what he knew, by showing her
respect and tenderness and consideration.
A sorry change, indeed, from what he had
fondly fancied that their united lots would
be! He almost laughed aloud in his
despair. The stable clock struck one. He
had actually been sitting there for two
hours or more.

The damp sticks were now no longer
alight, and the room was very chilly. The
sleet had changed to snow, and the flakes
were floating past the windows, melting on
the cornices of the house, and soaking into
the shrubbery paths. Frank recognized
Anthony's cheerful voice in the hall, talking
to Renée. How happy he seemed, and yet
—and yet he too had married a woman
very superior in every way to him, whom

many men might have loved and tried to take away. Frank rose and stretched himself wearily. Then he struck a match and burnt the letter in the grate, watching it until not a fragment remained.

"Never in any case say, 'I *have lost* such a thing, *but I have returned it*. . . . Is thy wife dead? it is a return—I am content that I have used thy gifts so long. Take them again, and set them in what place thou wilt, for thine were all things, and thou gavest them me!'" "Ah!" thought Frank, as these words that he had lately read came back to him, "the wise of all ages, Greek and Jew and Christian, have said the same. We cannot expect to keep and hold anything long. The sooner we understand this fact of life and bear its results like men, the better for us. I have been very happy, little Léo, for—how long is it?—a year. I will be patient then, during decades of loneliness, if they must come."

As in a dream, Hesseltine listened to the conversation of his host and hostess, sitting together in the dining-room. He helped Jos to collect the usual midday meal for the birds; he attended, in appearance courteously, but without understanding one syllable, to Tony's explanation of why the boiler had leaked, and how they could still manage to get hot water for baths if they wanted it; and when Renée, who had been looking inquiringly at him from time to time, asked him if he was prepared to go down to the village tea and concert, he willingly acquiesced. The truth was that he almost dreaded being left alone again just yet. He could more easily, he thought, play the part which he had determined upon, if he did not dwell too much quite at first on this never-ending sorrow. Mrs. Gore had noted the expression of his face when he had come down-stairs, she knew that he had read the letter, that his love had received a death-wound, and one that he was determined to bear in patience and silence. Her vengeance on Léo was complete. Yet her conscience smote her somewhat when she saw the suffering of the man who had been such a true friend to her, and she honestly wished that she could have punished her rival in a way that would have affected her alone. But unfortunately none such had seemed possible.

At about four o'clock the Gores and their guest started for the village tea, held in a large iron room that the late squire had put up for meetings, concerts, and other harmless rural dissipations. Mrs. Pettifer, in her best rustling black silk, was already becoming heated over the preparations. She was standing surrounded by a mountain of slices of plum-cake, a chaos of buns, and hunks of buttered bread. Large brown urns stood at the end of each narrow table. The youngest Master Pettifer was being

carried about by his sister, a slender girl
with projecting teeth, the image of what
her mother had been before she had grown
careworn and prematurely old. Mr. Pettifer, closely followed by Anthony's godson,
a very ugly boy of seven summers, was
carrying piles of blue and white crockery,
and picking his way among the cut bread
and butter spread out in dishes on the
floor. The school teachers were giggling
with the organist and the young man who
played the concertina. The sight of the
hot room and the warmer people passing to
and fro gave Frank an indescribable feeling
of gloom and disgust, though he was as
a rule philanthropically disposed enough.
Anthony, however, was cheerful and voluble
in conversation, and stumbled gaily about
among the dishes, upsetting some, and
apologizing profusely every time that he
did so.

"Oh, Mr. Gore, you are dragging the

table-cloth off!" cried Mrs. Pettifer in
despair, looking hot and wearied in her
crackling black silk. "Your elbow has
caught in it! Oh, goodness me, the urn
was nearly overturned. It gave me quite
a shock. Mrs. Gore, we thought *you* would
like a nice quiet tea in the corner, so Jessie
and Maud and Miss Pringle are cutting
some thin slices for you. All right, Tommy,
don't drag at my skirt; that's a good boy.
Thanks, Mr. Adamson, yes, when we've put
that table ready, I think we might begin!"

A long file of children, mostly wearing
hob-nailed boots and magenta comforters,
came tramping in, and a grace was sung.
The room soon became curiously steamy, it
seemed to Frank. He watched Renée's
graceful figure moving about among the
tables, and Anthony's hulking shoulders
towering above the school-master and Mr.
Pettifer. The clergyman's wife, administer-
ing alternately tea and mild reproofs to the

children, presided at one table, her daughter
with the prominent teeth at another. Frank,
in the midst of his own sadness, noticed how
tired the girl looked.

"Let me help you," he said kindly.
"Your arms must ache with handing cups.
I'll take them round."

Miss Pettifer looked up, surprised and
touched.

"I *am* tired," she said; "and I've got
such a dreadful attack of neuralgia. I
always have it when it's cold and damp
like to-day."

"Doesn't anything do it good?"

"I haven't time to try," she said, with
a half smile. Considering that she was
governess, nurse, and sometimes housemaid
as well, that she sat up late at night
darning stockings and mending children's
frocks, this was certainly very true. Frank
looked at her compassionately. And the
room grew more and more stifling, and

Anthony's voice louder and harsher as he
walked up and down chaffing the teachers,
complimenting the children on their appe-
tites, and giving friendly advice to Mr. and
Mrs. Pettifer.

At last another grace was sung, the
children ran shouting into the school-yard,
and the clergyman's wife, with loosened
bonnet-strings and a flushed nose, gave a
sigh of relief. Windows were flung open,
benches moved, and a row of chairs arranged
on the platform for the chorus singers. The
cottage-piano was dragged a little more
forward, and a young lady in white kid
gloves undid a roll of music.

"Won't you go home now, Mr. Hesseltine?" said Renée, half amused, half
compassionate. "I am so sorry for you
being let in for this function! But I
warned you. *Tony*, now, loves it. He has
eaten half a plum-cake. And he doesn't
dislike a frowsty room, for it never gives

him a headache. The singing will be the most terrible part—*do* go home!"

Frank hesitated. "I don't suppose the programme is a very long one? And I shall enjoy the walk home with you. I'll stop."

The school-master was meanwhile making the evening hideous with the tuning of his fiddle, and the young lady was taking off her white kid gloves. Mr. Pettifer clambered on to the platform, the choir-boys with shiny cheeks sat down on the row of chairs, and a few opening chords were struck.

"Miss Pettifer," said the vicar, "will give us a song." And his weary-looking daughter, naturally nervous, but more so than ever this evening, from pain and fatigue, opened a sheet of music with trembling fingers. It was a poor perform- ance enough, the singer's voice dying away altogether once or twice, and cracking at a high note. But Frank applauded loudly with his walking-stick on the floor. He had a fellow-feeling for every one to-night who looked oppressed and sad and hopeless. The little refrain—

"White wings, they never grow weary!"

pleased the audience, for they shouted "Ong-core" more than once.

"Must I sing again, papa?" asked the poor girl.

"Capital, capital, Miss Pettifer," shouted Anthony. "That's a first-class toon. Sing us another. The one about the 'Lady's Bower.' That's a ripper."

Miss Pettifer sang again, pressing her hand to her aching forehead once or twice, and was followed by a concertina solo from the distinguished amateur before alluded to. Then Mr. Pettifer's eldest son, a lank-haired youth, with apparently but little sense of humour, gave a rendering of a popular music-hall stave, at which even Frank, with all his charity, could not force a smile.

"Mr. Adamson," the clergyman announced, "will now sing us a very old favourite, 'Ehren on the Rhine.'"

That last word made Hesseltine wince. He forgot the hot school-room, the indifferent songsters, even the lovely woman sitting beside him. His heart cried out for Léontine, his love, his wife, who had been his once among the roses in the garden by the Rhine. It mattered little that Mr. Adamson's voice was throaty, his enunciation faulty, for his song strangely affected Hesseltine in his present mood—

> " . . . We'll meet once more,
> At Ehren on the Rhine ! "

Would Léo and he be happy and together again one day in that sweet sunny land? Or would it never be well with them until a later day still—

> " When what is now is not,
> When all old faults and follies are forgot " ?

During the remainder of the village concert it did not signify to Frank Hesseltine whether the singing was flat or tuneful, whether *h*'s were left out in the words, or introduced unbidden. He only heard his wife's voice, not uplifted in song, but as if she were reading aloud the letter which he had found that morning—"Life would have been paradise. . . . We should have been absorbed in it. . . . Poor dear Frank . . . a man who has all my esteem."

He could almost have groaned aloud in his agony of mind.

"Do you feel the room hot, old chap?" Tony asked. "You look a bit pale. It *is* rather stuffy—all the people packed so close, you see. I like to watch their faces, they do enjoy themselves! Old Pettifer is a capital organizer, I must do him that credit. Why do you look at me, Renée, like that, and laugh? What did I say?"

"I only smiled because it is so satisfactory, my dear boy, to see how you amuse yourself. No one can say that your tastes are not innocent. Mr. Hesseltine and I are a shade more *blasés*. Thank Heaven, there's 'God save the Queen,' and we shall get out of this oven."

"Well, it's been a great success," said Anthony, genially slapping young Pettifer on the back. "Capital feed, and A 1 music. All the performers came out splendidly. We must hurry up now, Renée, or dinner 'll be too much cooked. Frank, you'll help my wife with her wraps? I must just have a word with the parson."

Side by side Mrs. Gore and Frank walked quickly home, the flickering lights of Crabston Hall being already visible at the first bend in the road. Neither of them felt much inclined for conversation, so it was almost a relief when Anthony arrived, with young Benjamin Pettifer in tow, announcing that he also would have dinner with them.

The following morning, Sunday, brought a letter to Frank from his wife. "She had found everything so comfortable in Carlton Gardens, and Louise Valendar would spend all Sunday there, and dine with her. She hoped to arrive at Ledsham on Tuesday, and should so enjoy a quiet time with Frank."

For the first time in his life, Hesseltine flung his wife's letter to him, after reading it once through, into the flames. As he watched the fire curling and darting round the sheets, he felt as though his old life was being burnt up with it. Outside the world looked very cold and silent, a thin coating of snow lying on the grass and the garden walls. He accompanied the Gores to church, walking hand in hand with Jos, whose volubility saved him the trouble of talking. The little boy explained at some length that he could not make up his mind whether he should be a coachman or a sailor when he grew up, and observed that

Jane, the nurse, thought he had better be a private gentleman, and do nothing. Then he informed Frank that it would be his birthday on Wednesday, and added that he wished Mr. Hesseltine could have stayed for it.

"I am afraid I can't, my little man; but you shall choose a present, and I will send it to you."

"I wish you *would* stay, Mr. Hesseltine," said Renée. "I am sure Léontine must be busy with shopping in London, and won't mind an extra day or two there."

He sighed.

"No, I dare say not. Well, I'll think it over."

The second post on Monday brought a note from Léontine to her husband, saying that she had caught a very bad cold, she supposed at the theatre on Saturday night, and would Frank object to her remaining on a day or two more in London?

"Well, you'll stay here then?" Renée

pleaded. "It *is* such a pleasure to us both."

And he agreed. He was awakened at about seven in the morning of Wednesday by little Jos dancing into his room, and clapping his hands.

"My birthday! my birthday!" he shouted.

Frank, only half awake, sat up.

"All right, old man, you'll find your present in the corner, wrapped up in brown paper."

And Jos, his curls flying, bore off his parcel in triumph. Frank felt sadder than ever when the little figure had flitted away. He positively dreaded the beginning of new days now. That afternoon he and Anthony rode over to the neighbouring county town, and met Lord Wheldale in the market-place. After the usual original remarks about the weather, the likelihood of frost, etc., Lord Wheldale observed—

"I had a glimpse of your wife, Hesseltine, on Saturday, at the St. James's Theatre. She was sitting just below us with some ladies, and Huddersfield. It is a first-rate play, very strong cast indeed."

Frank Hesseltine winced and bit his lip. The fates were certainly against poor Léontine, inasmuch as her having sat in the next stall to Lord Huddersfield was a mere accident. She had gone alone with Countess Valendar, and found that their seats were in the same row as those belonging to Lady Walter Percival and a lively party. But Hesseltine of course thought, "Ah! she has managed to meet him, as she said, just once more in London! Oh, Léo, Léo, a year's happiness is very short, with a lifetime of pain to follow!"

# CHAPTER XII.

LÉONTINE and her friend Countess
Valendar were sitting in the snug boudoir
belonging to the former young lady in
her luxurious home in Carlton Gardens.
It overlooked trees, now bare, but which
would soon burst into leafage, and become
the resort of twittering birds. In the
window were palms and ferns, poinsettias,
and arum-lilies, while numberless bouquets
of cut violets and narcissus made the air
almost too heavy with perfume. Léo,
looking paler and more tired than Louise
ever remembered to have seen her, was
lying back in a softly-cushioned chair, one

small foot in an elaborately embroidered shoe resting on a stool. A half-emptied tea-cup was beside her, for it was about five o'clock.

"It is delightful for me your having left your hotel and come here," said Léo.

"Still nicer for me, darling. When do you expect Mr. Hesseltine?"

"I am not quite sure. He is at Ledsham now, and old Lord Dullingham proposed himself there. Frank does not like to refuse to entertain him, as he was his father's greatest friend."

"Well, I hope you will pick up a little, Léo, before your Frank does appear. You are really much more ill with that cold than he knew. So feverish, my dear child, and that pulls you down. You seem dreadfully languid to-day."

"Do I? I am sorry if I am stupid. Shall you go out anywhere in the evening this week?"

"Only to a party at the Admiralty on Saturday, I think. I saw the Fortescues coming out of church, and they said I positively must come. But *you* ought not to go out at night as long as these cold winds last."

The footman here announced "Lady Mary Prosser," an unfortunate arrival at that particular moment, Countess Valendar having just lighted a second cigarette.

"How tired and pale you look, my dear Léontine!" said the new-comer, turning up her Shetland veil, and imprinting a kiss on Léo's white face.

"I have had a bad cold, and still feel rather weak."

"No wonder, my dear child, in this oppressive atmosphere! The flowers, I am sure, are giving off a quantity of carbonic acid gas! And the strong smell of smoke, too," with a glance at Countess Valendar, "cannot be wholesome! Daniel is not

much of a smoker, I rejoice to say, but
when he *does* indulge in a cigar, it is
*always* in his own sanctum ! "

Léo smiled. " I don't think it hurts
me. When did you come to London ? "

" Only a few days ago. Mamma's liver
has been dreadfully congested, poor dear,
but we can't get her to take exercise. She
will not go further than to the gate of
the square and back, though Dr. Dobson-
Bruce says she really must move. Papa,
however, has begun to do dumb-bells, and
is really wonderfully well, dear thing ! "

Countess Valendar had risen from her
seat, and was walking about the room.

" Are you looking for anything, Louise ? "

" Yes, for my little pack of cards."

" You surely," remonstrated Lady Mary,
" don't begin to play cards as early as
this ! I always think one can get through
so much reading and practising between
five and seven."

"I am going to tell fortunes," said Louise, laughing.

"You *cannot* really believe in such folly, my dear Countess Valendar!"

"Indeed I do. I am a wonderful prophet. Many of the things I have foretold have come sadly true! And some, on the other hand, were pleasant!"

"It seems to me quite wrong," said Lady Mary, with compressed lips. "Why do you put such ideas into Léontine's head? It *must* be absolute folly."

"Well, I am not so sure! I have prophesied some strange things. And do you know, I can tell the history of people who are *not* in the room by my cards, if I fix my thoughts on them, or hold one of their letters in my hand!"

"Well, it almost shocks me. I don't know what Daniel would say, Countess Valendar!"

"Shall I tell you all about his future *carrière?*"

"Please don't *think* of it. It is a dreadful idea."

"Here they are! here is my dear little pack!" cried the Countess. And she began shuffling the cards on her knee.

"I'm afraid no amount of good advice would eradicate all my superstitions, Lady Mary! How angry you would have been with me in the train coming from Queenborough! It was just starting, and I was about to shut the door of my compartment, when I saw a chimney-sweep, with a ladder, on the platform. I was out in a moment, though the guard stormed, and my maid was wild with agitation. I ran up to the sweep, and patted him, and got up to the step only the very moment the train moved out!"

"You might have broken your neck! How can you be so childish?"

"Well, I was in the best of spirits during the whole journey in consequence. And the same evening I also saw the new moon through an *open* window, over my right shoulder! So I expect no end of good luck!"

Lady Mary remained a little while longer, prescribing remedies for Léontine, and expressing her surprise, in rather marked tones, that Mr. Hesseltine was not with his wife. This last observation was the only one of Lady Mary's that really afforded any vexation to the patient Léo; especially as, almost in the same breath, her visitor asked her several leading questions about their visit to Crabston, and whether she knew if the Gores were coming shortly to London or no?

After Lady Mary's departure, Louise Valendar moved some books off her table, and spread out the cards.

"Well, Léo, whose future shall I tell? I have a great mind to give you some information about your dear little self!"

"Certainly, if you wish. But I am of the same mind as Lady Mary. I am an unbeliever."

Countess Valendar's face grew serious. She moved her table nearer to her friend's chair, and they went through the usual preliminaries of sorting and cutting the cards.

"Ah!" said Louise. "It is extraordinary! quite marvellous! the amount of love, and of money, and luck that I find in your life. Dear me! I never saw such cards."

Léontine smiled rather sadly.

"Luck and love and money! But I am an unbeliever, Louise, as you know."

"There are three men absolutely devoted to you!" cried the Countess. "I dare say there are lots more, but these are very conspicuous. One is going to make a long journey. And one is coming to your house very soon. Ah! there is a little hitch

here, Léo! there is a woman who comes
between you and one of the three men,
the man who is closest to you. There she
is, the Queen of Spades."

Léontine's face flushed, and she laughed
a forced laugh.

"There is always something about a
dark woman and a fair man. A gipsy
told me the same thing. It *is* nonsense,
dear Louise!"

But Countess Valendar, her forehead
puckered, her eyes bent upon the cards,
paid no attention to this remark.

"One of the three men will visit you
very soon, and probably bring you a
present. He is not quite as devoted as
the other two, but he is a very sincere
friend. Ah! a great change will come
over your life soon."

"Good or bad?" asked Léo, with the
same forced smile.

"Good, I rather think. But there *is*

some kind of disaster, connected with the dark woman, the Queen of Spades. One man will be very unhappy. Now, Léo, cut again."

Mrs. Hesseltine did so, and the Countess resumed,

"Now that *is* most astonishing! There she is again, that Queen, and always close to you in some odd way. I wonder—"

The footman interrupted the prophecies by announcing "Lord Strathmashie and Captain Sturgess." And the two gentlemen came in, the former changing colour a little as Léo shook hands with him.

"I was awfully sorry to hear you were seedy," he said. "Rotten weather just now, filthy east wind blows one about."

"We've heard of a marriage," said Captain Sturgess. "Three guesses, Mrs. Hesseltine. It's a friend of yours and Frank's."

"I can't imagine."

"It's good old Bill Huddersfield," said Strathmashie, without waiting for any guesses. "The bird's perched at last. Rum-looking girl, with sketchy kind of relations. But I believe he likes her."

"I am so glad. Is it Miss MacGwire Jones?"

"That's it. Saw her walking with her father, an extraordinary old buster, and Billy with them in tow."

"Is she very rich?" asked Countess Valendar, much excited. "What is the father?"

"An old stumer-spotter from Liverpool, I believe."

"A *what?*" cried the Countess.

"He means a banker," said Sturgess, laughing. "Strath's English isn't very easy for Germans, or even some of his own compatriots to understand. I must say I never thought Huddersfield would make up his mind to settle down. I

dare say he'll be a very good husband,
though. And he'll be able to astonish Mr.
MacGwire Jones, if he feels inclined."

"I am really very pleased," said Léontine.
And she added in a low voice, "There *is*
a great deal of good in Lord Huddersfield."

As the young men rose to depart,
Strathmashie, blushing again, said "he had
left some violets for Mrs. Hesseltine in the
hall. But she had so many lovely flowers
and plants he was sure they'd only be in
the way."

"It is so kind of you!" Léontine's
smile would have been reward enough for a
far more important gift. And so, perhaps,
Strathmashie thought.

"Ah, Léo," cried Countess Valendar, as
the steps died away below. "I said you
were to have a visitor and a present from
one of your admirers! It is our young
friend with the high collar and the beautiful
white silk tie!"

"Nonsense, Louise, you always imagine that every one is devoted to me." She paused a little. "But you are entirely wrong sometimes."

When Léo had gone up-stairs to rest, Countess Valendar sat on awhile at her card-table, her face wearing a very puzzled expression.

"What has happened?" she asked herself. "Something has gone very wrong with Léo, and I cannot for the life of me imagine what it is. She is more sad than ill, and that is why she looks so white and fagged. I am almost sure, poor darling, that I heard her sobbing and crying last night. But I don't feel as if I could ask about it, as she evidently wishes me to know nothing. It is very strange; she has been married just a year, to a man of high character, who certainly would have no kind of *liaison* after marriage, and who was desperately devoted to her. I never saw any one more

in love. Can it be that she feels *she* has
made a mistake? Good Heavens! she must
have got over that stupid fancy for that
scamp Huddersfield! And she wrote me
such happy letters after her marriage. It
is inexplicable. It only shows how little
one can judge for other people. Those
two seemed to have every earthly thing
to make them happy—looks and health,
money and popularity, and I thought
mutual affection."

Countess Valendar was no nearer arriving
at a solution of her perplexities after Frank's
arrival two days later in Carlton Gardens.
She had yielded to Léo's assurances that
she would not be in the least in the way
if she remained on as the Hesseltines' guest.
" On the contrary," said Léontine, " it would
be a genuine pleasure to Frank to find his
old friend still there."

Louise happened to be in the boudoir
when Mr. Hesseltine walked in. During

the morning she had noticed that Léontine seemed agitated and restless, as much as pleased, at the prospect of her husband's arrival. But the greeting between the two was anything but lover-like. Frank kissed his wife lightly on the forehead, asked her in rather an indifferent manner a few questions as to the state of her health, and then sitting down by Countess Valendar, he began to talk, with rather forced cheerfulness, about current affairs. Louise glanced hastily at Léo. She saw that every vestige of colour had left her cheeks, and that she looked anxious and worried. Decidedly there was a curious constraint between the husband and wife.

"Have you been very busy at Ledsham, Frank?" asked Léo, with an odd pleading expression in her eyes that Countess Valendar could not understand.

"Well, I'm never very idle there. I had old Wordie over, and we arranged some autographs. Have you been seeing any one interesting?"

"Well, we saw Lady Mary. She gave us good advice, didn't she, Louise?"

"The very best, as usual. By the way, Mr. Hesseltine, will you be my chaperon to the party at the Admiralty to-morrow? I tell Léo she ought not to go out yet on these cold nights."

"I shall be charmed. Oh, Léo, I heard that the Gores were to come to London to-day."

Léontine started, and did not answer. She turned her head away, and began moving some little glass vases full of violets.

"Yes," continued Frank, "they are coming for about a week. At least, Tony is. Mrs. Gore may remain longer. Her brother, little Jos's father, is home on leave from Malta, and he has taken a flat in London for a short time. So Mrs. Gore will be there a good deal, I dare say. She don't

like being parted long from Jos. I hope
you are not going to hurry away from
England, my dear Countess?"

"Well, I don't know. My sick relation
is better, but I still linger on in London,
you see. It is capital that you will take
me to-morrow to the party."

Louise Valendar found but little opportunity of speaking to her host alone. But
on the following morning at breakfast,
before Léo came down, she observed—

"Doesn't it strike you that Léontine
looks ill? To me she seems ever so much
thinner. Perhaps she wants a thorough
change."

"She can always go wherever she likes."

Something in his tone surprised Countess
Valendar.

"She would not care to go away by
herself!"

"Oh, I would take her anywhere she
fancied, of course. But surely she has

variety enough. We shall be leaving for Yorkshire soon."

"I felt rather depressed about her a day or two ago."

"I suppose it is the result of this bad cold," said Frank. "Will you excuse me opening this letter?"

"It's a pity we went to that play," continued Countess Valendar. "It was horribly cold waiting till we got the carriage. I should have been quite happy spending a quiet evening here, but Léo seemed bent on the theatre."

Frank looked up quickly. "It *was* unfortunate!" he said drily. And then with a change of tone, "Oh, by the way, I hear Huddersfield is going to be married."

"Yes, indeed. I rather pity poor Miss MacGwire Jones. But if ever man has had his fling—isn't that your expression?—Lord Huddersfield has."

"I certainly don't think Miss Jones is to

be envied.   I suppose his debts are very pressing."

"So his friends seem to think.   Ah! here is dear Léo!   Are you rested, darling? What an adorable dress you have got on!"

Léontine looked at her husband, hoping, perhaps, for a word of commendation from him too.   But he was silent, and pushed away his coffee-cup.

"I am going to leave you two ladies to gossip," he said, "and do a little work.   I very likely shan't be in for luncheon, Léo. Anthony Gore has just written to ask me to lunch with him at his club.   And I am dining out—a very dull dinner, with some men who only talk business.   I will come in the brougham and fetch you at 10.30, Countess, if that suits you, for the Admiralty party?"

"Léo, you really must try and eat a little more.   You only play with your food," said Countess Valendar, a few minutes later.

" I don't ever feel hungry now."

" Well, then, see a doctor. It is foolish to let yourself go down like this." But Louise's advice had no result, for Léontine's breakfast went, almost untasted, down-stairs.

Punctually at half-past ten that evening, the Countess, having smoked a last cigarette, and put on her magnificent sables, got into Mr. Hesseltine's brougham, and the two drove off to the Admiralty. She there met so many friends, old and new, that during the course of the evening she saw very little of Frank. Presently the new German Ambassador came up, and asked her the name of a beautiful lady dressed in pale yellow, with very fine diamonds.

Louise followed the direction of his eyes, and recognized Mrs. Gore, in earnest conversation with Hesseltine. Later on in the evening Countess Valendar noticed them again together in the tea-room, and once more in the hall, where a large concourse of people were awaiting their carriages. Anthony Gore came up and did his best to make himself agreeable to Louise, until an old man with a tuft of white hair and a very red face startled him by giving him a violent thump on his back.

"Hallo, Admiral!" said Tony. "Fancy you here! When did you come to London?"

"Jane and I are up for a week," said Admiral Mullins, "but it's uncommon poor fun in this weather. A fog down one's throat one day, and an east wind going through one's bones on the next. But this ain't a bad party, I must say."

The Admiral was in good spirits, having succeeded in button-holing the First Lord for a good five minutes, and the Commander - in - Chief from Portsmouth for another ten. Miss Mullins was meekly waiting in a thorough draught for a four-wheeler. A wisp of unloosened hair and an uncurled blue ostrich feather drooped upon her neck. In the middle of the back of her fur-lined circular cloak a large ticket was pinned, inscribed with the number "50." The Admiral caught sight of it, nudged Mr. Gore, and broke into peals of hilarious laughter, interspersed with coughing.

"D'ye see that? Look at Jane's back— ha! ha! That's uncommon funny. She ain't quite fifty yet, but she's doosid near it! I say, Jenny, put your hand up and feel your back. It ain't no use now, you're sitting in the 'dusk with the light behind yer.' You're labelled, and you can't get out of it. Ha, ha!"

Frank Hesseltine came down the steps with Renée just as Countess Valendar, whose manners were charming, removed the ticket from Miss Mullins's back, and kindly begged her to come out of the draught. When Louise turned her head, she saw that Mrs. Gore and her host were again engrossed with one another, and for the first time a melancholy suspicion darted into her mind.

Admiral Mullins was enchanted to see Mr. Hesseltine again, and was profuse in his inquiries for Léontine. "She can play whist, she can. She's got an old head on young shoulders! I say, there's a man I want a word with."

Admiral Mullins had espied the figure of the newly-made Comptroller of the Navy entering the supper-room, and was after him like a dog on the track of a hare. The last-named distinguished officer was, however, too quick for him, and had ensconced himself with a very pretty lady at a round table in a far corner, where it was difficult for Admiral Mullins to follow. Baffled in his quest, the Admiral helped himself to a tumbler of champagne out of a jug, and went back into the hall, to find the footman, the linkman, and Miss Mullins in agitated colloquy about his four-wheeler, in which he shortly drove away with his daughter.

On the following day Louise Valendar again produced her little pack of cards. Léontine had been to the Oratory, had felt very tired at luncheon, and was now gone up-stairs, so that the Countess was left alone until Lord Strathmashie put in an appearance. His face fell considerably when he was informed that Mrs. Hesseltine was not well enough to come down.

"What the dickens are you doing?" he asked of Countess Valendar. "Playing patience?"

"Oh dear, no, nothing so frivolous. No game at all, but something very serious. Shall I go on?"

"Certainly; I want to see the sport."

"I repeat, it is very serious. Don't talk for a minute, please, because I must think earnestly of a person who is now absent."

She closed her eyes for a few seconds, shuffled, cut, and became absorbed in the cards.

"Dear me! This is the most extraordinary thing! They are so very much like the last time. Only I see more disaster now."

Strathmashie began to be interested.

"Yes, there are three men, and here's the one who is nearest to her. Something will happen, because of that woman who comes between. Now I must do the second part, shuffle and cut again."

Lord Strathmashie employed the interval in staring very hard at a photograph of Léontine.

"Well, I was never more astonished!" cried the Countess. "The plot thickens in a most extraordinary way. The fair man—"

"Which is that Johnny?"

"The King of Hearts. He is gone further off now. But the woman who divides my friend from the other man is still here, quite close."

"I call that devilish uncanny," said Lord Strathmashie.

"Well, it *is* most curious. I have set my heart on finding out about this person whose fate I now tell."

"So have I," said the young man, edging his chair a little nearer. "Though, you'll forgive me for saying it, I consider it all rot."

"Never mind. Shuffle once more. There she is now, that Queen of Spades again! But further off, in a different row, Lord Strathmashie. That's a good thing, my friend. Do you know, I've got a notion that I know who that Queen of Spades means! She is a very dangerous woman to have for an enemy. Ah! you smile; do you know whom I am alluding to? Who is the Queen of Spades?"

"I've got a pretty shrewd guess," said Lord Strathmashie.

# CHAPTER XIII.

Mr. Anthony Gore was in the best of
spirits. He was about to entertain a large
party at Crabston Hall for a Primrose
League Meeting in the neighbouring town,
and had secured the services of the well-
known orator, Mr. Prosser, Q.C., M.P.
for the Muddiford Boroughs, as principal
speaker. For ten days or more—ever since
his return from London, in fact—Anthony
had been busily employed in visiting his
own tenants, the local tradesmen, the licensed
victuallers of the neighbourhood, and a

good many of the labourers, or those of
each class, to be more accurate, who wore
the primrose badge, or were supposed to
take an interest in the Conservative cause.
Anthony not being personally endowed with
the gift of eloquence, had laid out a
considerable sum in the purchase of political
pamphlets, which he distributed with a
lavish hand. He now usually started early
in the morning, on horseback, to pay a
series of calls, and to urge upon his neighbours the importance of not missing the
coming opportunity of listening to the great
politician. He was often disheartened at
the want of interest shown by them both
in the present state of Ireland and in
Egyptian affairs; but, on the other hand,
Mr. Prosser's *brochure* on the land question
was tolerably well appreciated; and one or
two stolid yokels even volunteered a wish
to go and hear him speak for himself.

One evening, Anthony, wearing very

muddy boots and bespattered gaiters, strode into the rose-coloured drawing-room at Crabston Hall, in which his wife was busily employed in arranging a high glass with boughs and ivy trails. Renée had been singularly silent and out of spirits since her return from London, almost morose at times, and her want of enthusiasm both as to the expected house-party and the political meeting would have been seriously damping to the ardour of any one less amiable and more observant than Mr. Gore. The news of Huddersfield's projected marriage had fallen like a thunder-clap upon Renée. Her first outburst of passionate grief was changing now into a state of sullen despair; but she was proud and self-controlled enough not to betray her feelings to the outside world otherwise than by being a little more sarcastic than usual, and more uncivilly intolerant of people who bored her.

"I say, old girl," cried Tony, "I *have* had a day of it! I started at nine thirty sharp, rode about three hours over the country, took a bit of lunch at Chalk Farm, trotted off to Sparston and Paxton, and then came back through the town and had a word with Heckingthorpe at the station, and Battye at the King's Arms. Oh, by the way, they say we ought to put up more notices and posters! Now, how would *you* word them, my old darling? You're much sharper than I am. I want something to catch the eye, don't you know."

"Why don't you have a row of sandwich-men with '*Prosser is coming!*' on the boards, or '*The Great Prosser!*' You might dress the men up in some eccentric costume — primrose colour, perhaps, with bouquets of flowers!"

"Don't chaff, Renée; I really want to know what you think."

"Or you might stick up bills with

' *Who's Prosser?* ' on them. I am sure very few people would be able to tell you."

Tony's honest face fell.

" I wish you wouldn't turn the whole thing into ridicule," he said sadly.

" You might also add, ' *Prosser, the safe man.*' He certainly comes under that heading ; he is not likely ever to set the Thames on fire."

Renée took up a long trail of variegated creeper, and began twisting it round the stem of her high glass. Poor Anthony was now walking impatiently up and down the room.

" You're very provoking, Renée ! I should have thought you'd have taken *some* little interest in your first large house-party. We've got such a nice lot of people together too. Should we draw lots at dinner after the first night ? "

" If you like. There is a certain grim

humour in a person like Mr. Prosser going in as 'Romeo,' with Miss Mullins, for instance, as 'Juliet.'"

"You're coming with me into the town to-morrow, aren't you, Renée?" said her husband, seeing that it was useless to attempt serious discussion. "I want you so much, there's a dear, to call on one or two people who are rather huffy, and ask them to come to the meeting. I make such stupid mistakes. I thought a man was a 'Harbinger,' and he turned out to be a bigger swell. Now *you* never put your foot in it."

Mr. Gore began to whistle 'Rule Britannia' very loudly. After a pause he said—

"Have you heard from Jos to-day? Poor little chap! I dare say he wishes himself back at Crabston. London's a dull place for a boy."

"He wrote two days ago; he has been to a circus, and the Zoo. How I wish he were back here!" And Mrs. Gore sighed wearily.

"You're a bit tired," said Anthony, kindly, patting his wife's shoulder. "I'm sorry if I bored you, old girl, about all this business. But some one must make plans."

The following afternoon Mrs. Gore went up to her room an hour or so before she and her husband were to start for their drive to the neighbouring town. Her face looked, for her, drawn and pale, and when she was left alone she made no effort to control herself any longer. She covered her eyes with one hand, and the tears trickled quickly through her fingers—tears of anger as much as of pain. After a few moments she rose, and lifted a despatch-box full of letters on to a high chair. She opened it, and drew out a large packet of letters, a hundred or more, securely tied with a ribbon. Some were notes of a few words, others were closely-written sheets.

They had been taken out of their envelopes, and were carefully arranged according to date, some of them having been written several years back, others very recently. It was over the latter letters, some twenty, that Mrs. Gore lingered, reading and re-reading one or two, while a curious expression, half of sorrow, half of triumph, flitted over her eyes and brow. Once or twice she pressed the sheets to her lips and kissed them. A loud voice calling her from below broke in upon her reverie.

"Renée! Renée, old girl! The trap's there. Look sharp!"

Mrs. Gore started to her feet. Some of the letters lay on the table, others upon her knee. She was sitting at an old-fashioned writing bureau, containing numberless small drawers and recesses. Into one of the former she put all the letters.

"I shall be only a couple of hours away," she thought. "Not a soul comes in here, or ever touches my writing-table. Then, when I come in, I will read them—oh, God! why do I torture myself like this?—once again and arrange them carefully, or burn them . . . . if I can. Billy, Billy—have you quite forgotten all the things you said to me here?"

"Renée—Renée!" cried the voice from below again. And Mr. Gore's heavy footfall was now heard coming up-stairs.

"All right, Tony. How you bother me! I shall be ready in two seconds!"

Anthony burst open the door and entered.

"Well, you *are* an old slow coach! I have got an appointment with the Mayor, and he's the sort of chap who gets a bit touchy if one isn't punctual. Come on!"

Mr. and Mrs. Gore drove along the muddy roads for some three miles, inspected the Town Hall, where the meeting was to be held, and visited the Mayor and Mayoress, and a few other local celebrities.

" We'll go and have a cup o' tea at
the Red Lion," said Anthony ; "after two
hours' jawing and doing the civil, one feels
thirsty. Hallo! there's Pettifer coming
towards us."

Mr. Pettifer advanced, and took off his
squashy felt hat to Mrs. Gore.

" I have driven into the town with Dr.
Bains," he said. " And I went up to the
Hall first, as I wanted to have a word with
you on business, Gore. I found this telegram
for Mrs. Gore, so brought it on with me,
in case it should be important."

He handed the orange envelope to Renée.
The colour died away out of her cheeks as
she read the contents.

" Oh, Tony—Tony! he's so dreadfully
ill! I must go to him at once!"

Her husband snatched the ominous missive
out of her hands. It was a telegram from
Jos's father, saying that the boy was
dangerously ill, and that Renée had better

come immediately to London. Anthony's kind face clouded over. He was very sincerely fond of little Jos.

"It is hard luck," he said, his lip quivering. "Look here, old girl," and he took out his watch as he spoke, "if you don't mind having your maid and your luggage sent after you, you could catch the five thirty-five train from *here*, and be in London almost in time for dinner. We can get a fly in two minutes at this hotel."

"Oh, Tony, how sharp of you to remember that! I'll go at once. Order the fly as quickly as ever you can."

"I am truly sorry," said Mr. Pettifer; "but we must hope for the best. Jos is a strong little fellow, and he'll pull through, with God's help."

The vicar sighed as he spoke, remembering a fair-haired little boy of his own who had passed out of this troublesome world when he was just the age of Jos.

Renée was in a fever of impatience until the fly came to the door.

"I'll see you to the station, old girl. We've got lots of time. I dare say you can rub along without your luggage till to-morrow morning? Oh, I say, Renée, the people were to arrive the day after to-morrow; shall I put them off?"

"No, no. Oh, Tony, don't think of the worst. He *must*, he shall get better. There is no reason why you shouldn't have the party without me. It will disappoint a lot of people if you don't!"

"All right," said Anthony, ruefully. "But it'll all be flat and horrid without you. I am such a stupid sort of chap. I shan't be able to amuse 'em."

"Oh, yes, you will. It will be all right. You see they only stay two nights. I will wire to you how my darling is as soon as I get to London."

Anthony Gore, looking very melancholy,

watched the train steam out of the station.
Almost all his pleasurable anticipation re-
garding his party was at an end. He was
a little consoled, however, when at nine
o'clock a telegram from Renée reached him,
saying, " Dangerously ill ; but doctor says
may still hope. Shall remain for the
present."

During the first half-hour of her journey
Mrs. Gore had had no thought for any
one or anything excepting the child who
might be sick unto death. Suddenly, however, she remembered with a pang the very
compromising letters which she had left in
the drawer of her writing-table. She tried,
however, to put aside all anxiety, by telling
herself that no one would ever dream of
touching her possessions, for clearly it was
impossible to have them sent on to her, or
to give any directions, which might excite
curiosity concerning them. But in spite of
all her efforts to bring quiet to her mind,

she could not avoid an occasional feeling of dread, or a notion—for she was naturally superstitious — that all these events had occurred in the course of a judgment upon her.

Tony, meanwhile, smoked his solitary pipe, read the *Field, Land and Water*, and two chapters of "*Jorrocks*," stretched himself, and finally went to sleep in an arm-chair with his mouth wide open.

The next morning he received another fairly reassuring telegram from London, so felt that he might, with an easy conscience, continue his preparations. He interviewed the cook, giving way at last to her suggestion that fish must positively be ordered from London for the two nights, and the pike for once cease to appear—strolled into the bedrooms at all hours, thereby worrying the housemaids to no small extent — and finally ordered his horse so as to ride over and have another look at the Town Hall.

In the Market Place he met Lord Wheldale, and stopped to have a little conversation with him. The idea suddenly flashed across Anthony's mind, that in his wife's absence it was a pity not to use her lovely blue room, and thereby at the same time do a civility to a very friendly neighbour.

"I say!" he remarked, "couldn't you and Lady Wheldale and Lady Katie come and stay at Crabston to-morrow for a brace o' nights? Delighted to put you up. You might like to meet Prosser? He knows what he's talking about. I expect he'll draw like anything here."

"I really think we might manage it," said Lord Wheldale cheerfully. "I'll ask my Lady, and send over a man with a note."

And the result of this interview was that Lord and Lady Wheldale and their daughter expressed themselves as delighted to accept Mr. Gore's kind invitation. On receipt of this note, Tony and the housekeeper had a long and earnest discussion about the arrangement of the bedrooms, arriving finally at the conclusion that Lady Mary Prosser should occupy Mrs. Gore's pretty blue room.

"We mustn't let her think it isn't a spare room," said Tony. "We'll clear out all the books and photographs, and odds and ends."

This was done so effectually that Lady Mary, when she was shown into the blue room, had no idea whatsoever that it was usually occupied by the wife of her host.

The first dinner really went off very well, in spite of Mr. Gore's evident nervousness. Mr. Prosser was full of conversation, and found himself quite in accord with Lord Wheldale as to his political views. Admiral Mullins was likewise in high good-humour, and delighted with Lady Katie's pretty face and manners. The other country

neighbours, and an old college friend of
Anthony's, were all determined to make
themselves pleasant to their kindly host,
the more so as he had to entertain them
without his wife's help. Lady Wheldale
was full of admiration for the decoration
and colouring of the rooms, and profuse in
her regrets at Mrs. Gore's absence. Lady
Mary, dressed in a satin gown of a crude
shade of lilac-pink, gave good advice to
her host and to any one else who would
listen to her with patience. Anthony
judiciously put a veto upon the suggestion
of playing whist in the evening, although
the Admiral expressed himself as anxious
for a rubber.

"We'd better all turn in early to-night,"
said Mr. Gore. "You've got a hard evening before you, Prosser, to-morrow."

The success of the Primrose League
Meeting, when it did eventually take place,
exceeded Anthony's most sanguine expecta-

tions. Mr. Prosser, Q.C., spoke fluently for an hour and a half, and afterwards replied with amiable playfulness to the serious or bantering questions put to him by his audience. The Mayor, who was chairman on the occasion, made a few eloquent remarks at the close of the meeting, proposing a vote of thanks to their distinguished guest, and the proceedings concluded without a hitch.

Every one congratulated Mr. Gore on the result of his trouble and energy.

"I only wish my wife had been here," he said. "It would have been ever so much cheerier for you all. But I hope you haven't been awfully bored at Crabston?"

"Indeed we've had a charming visit! It was *so* pleasant and nice, Mr. Gore! So kind of you to ask us!"

The Squire stood bareheaded on the steps, as one by one the guests descended, to get into flys. The green landau was in waiting for Lady Mary and her Q.C.; and the Wheldales' carriage had arrived to take them home.

"A thousand thanks, my dear Mr. Gore, for a most enjoyable and profitable visit," said Mr. Prosser. "My dear wife and I greatly appreciate your hospitality."

"Yes, indeed!" chimed in Lady Mary. "And—oh, Mr. Gore, I thought I ought to give you these—I have wrapped them up very untidily, I fear—letters that I found in the writing-table in that charming old-fashioned bureau! It occurred to me that some previous guest might have left them. And of course they wouldn't like the idea. So I entrust them to you. Thanks again for our most agreeable visit. And give my kindest regards to your wife."

Mr. Prosser, rather ostentatiously, put a sovereign into the butler's hand, and followed Lady Mary into the carriage.

"Well, so that's all over!" soliloquized

Anthony, as his eyes followed the last departing wheels. "Hallo! the paper's come off these letters, and I've dropped one. They must be my girl's. What a lot, all in one writing! I wonder who her correspondent is—a pretty constant one!"

Mr. Gore began to whistle his favourite air, "I'll meet her when the sun goes down," and cheerfully examined the letters.

The whistle stopped abruptly. His face had suddenly grown quite blanched, with a curious expression, half of fear, half of anger, in his eyes. He was standing now on the identical spot where, not long ago, Frank Hesseltine had discovered another letter which had as deeply affected him. Mr. Gore strode quickly across the hall, and went into the smoking-room. His fox-terrier sprang up from the rug, and rubbed his head against Anthony's knees. His master patted him mechanically. Then he threw himself down into one of the large

leather-covered arm-chairs near the fire.
His square hands trembled as he spread out
the sheets. His face looked like that of a
man undergoing terrible physical torture,
but who was determined to die before he
gave vent to a groan. The cold perspiration ran down his forehead. He read, very
slowly — Anthony Gore had never been
quick at taking things in—one letter after
another, all dated Aldershot. At first the
dates had puzzled him. It must have been
a mistake! They could *not* have been
written such a little while ago! One or
two sentences sent all the blood back into
his gray face — passionate expressions of
endearment, which yet seemed to him,
stupid as he was, to have a ring of con-
tempt in them. Then he read other letters,
of an earlier date, each one wringing his
kind and trusting heart afresh. And finally
he sprang up, as a wild beast may spring,
when he sees a shrinking animal cowering

before him, and dashed his hand down upon a table, grazing the skin till the blood came.

He spoke out loud, in a voice quite unlike his own.

"If it had been any other man, some one clever, some one who knows more than me ; but *he*, why he is no better than the biggest fool of us all ! Nothing but his handsome face, damn him !"

Anthony Gore tore open his collar. He felt a longing for fresh air. And, staggering as he went, he crossed the room to the window and flung it open.

"She *can't* have thought what it would be to me ! She can't have known how I loved her ! *Loved !*—why, I still do. But if I could only have five minutes with him, I'd break his blasted neck for him ! "

The notion that Huddersfield had again and again kissed the face that was so passionately dear to him would obtrude itself. Then he walked up and down, up and down the room, in the madness of his grief, only stopping now and again to look at his wife's picture. At last he rang the bell.

"I am going out," he said shortly to the servant who answered it. "I shall want no luncheon."

He fetched his hat and stick, and, followed by his dog, strode out of the house. For miles and miles he walked, through muddy lanes, over bleak fields, past stretches of bare uncultivated ground; impelled to go on—on, he knew not where; but only so that he must become utterly wearied, and thus deaden a little the gnawing mental pain that seemed likely to unhinge his mind. The idea of treachery was something unknown to Anthony Gore, whose own life had been of the simplest and straightest; the notion of dishonour in his own home was so strange to him as to be stupefying. The sky was growing overcast, the evening drawing in. He noticed how tired the little dog looked, and stooping, picked him up in his arms. During that pause Anthony glanced at the lurid sky to westward. It seemed to him like some infernal region, in which the black boughs of the trees standing out against it were as arms of demons beckoning to him. He shuddered and strode onwards, holding the dog against his breast. As he passed by a small village the church clock struck, and he realized how long he had been walking. Want of food and great mental anguish had made him at last utterly exhausted, and he slowly retraced his steps. On arriving at home, he said that he would want no dinner, only some coffee in his bedroom; for he felt that he could not as yet sit down quietly and face the curious eyes of the old servants.

Through all the terrible night that followed, Anthony Gore, tired out as he was, never slept. He lay pondering, still half dazed at the extraordinary change that had come over his simple, prosperous life; wondering whether it could really be he, himself, who was doomed to this awful awakening. Certainly the elements of tragedy had never as yet entered into poor Anthony's existence. It had all been so humdrum, so calm, so respectable. Looking back on it, he probably exaggerated its happiness. His father had often been cross and irritable; his mother, in spite of strong religious principles and good intentions, sometimes hard and unsympathetic. His only sister had been married long ago, and was living far away at an Indian station. His holidays as a boy at home had not really been particularly lively, his career at Oxford not crowned with much success; yet there was now a curious sort of glamour over all this poor dead past. What would his mother, with her straight and narrow notions; his father, with his old-fashioned rigid codes, have said to this end of their son's life? For to Anthony Gore there was now no longer anything to desire, anything to live for. He had given his whole self to this beautiful cruel woman who had deceived him all along. But it never occurred to him to hate or even to despise her. His only vindictive feelings were for the man who had won what was denied to him. Towards morning he rose, dressed himself, and went out again, having tasted nothing; and it was only when faintness threatened to overpower him that he came in. There was a letter from Renée for him on the table. He took it up to his own room, his lip twitching, and his knees shaking under him as he went. Then, without opening it, he sat down, worn out with misery, and cried as he had never cried since he was a little child.

# CHAPTER XIV.

## ANTHONY GORE GIVES A LESSON IN SHOOTING.

DURING his forty years of life Anthony Gore had not hitherto been specially remarkable for the quality of decision. He had usually taken a considerable time to make up his mind as to his conduct even on matters of minor importance. But now, strange to say, he did not hesitate to form a resolution which was by far the most serious that he had ever framed. His only difficulty at first was, as to the means by which it might be carried out. He had another long desolate day in which to mature his plans. After the receipt of his wife's letter, and the violent ebullition of grief before alluded to, he had become very calm, and outwardly almost cheerful again. He read, or appeared to read, his newspapers at luncheon, and ordered his horse to go for a long ride. Before starting he wrote two letters. The first was to his wife, and ran thus—

"I hardly know what I am saying, Renée, but I was always a stupid, dense fellow, and couldn't express myself very clearly. By accident, quite by accident,— for God knows I had no earthly suspicion about you, whom I have always held so dear,—some letters written to you by the biggest scoundrel unhung fell yesterday into my hands. I didn't think there was any harm in looking to see who they were from,—why should I? And—I read them. With what result on my mind you, who know what I have always felt about you, can guess. Life is over for me now, in one sense, all hope at least for the future ; so I think it had better really end altogether. No one but you will ever know that it isn't by a pure accident I am going to get out of this miserable world. When you read this I shall be gone ; and I don't feel afraid, my conscience doesn't tell me, somehow, that I am wrong. If I am, God forgive me, but I have been sorely tried. I leave you free to make your own life. I know—this is hardest of all for me to say—that the man who wrote those letters is bound to another woman ; but he could get out of that (I don't suppose he would hesitate) for your sake. I want you to know that I forgive you, entirely. Be happy in the future, Renée, *if you can.* Think of me just now and again as a man who, if he was a fool, and unworthy of you, loved you with his whole soul. And perhaps some day, if we ever meet again, you may get to care for me a little. Don't let little Jos forget me either. Please God, he'll soon be well, and have a happy life before him. I think I have said all I meant to. Oh, one thing more; look after the old servants. I have been thinking about the man who will come here after me, my cousin John Gore, now with his regiment in India. He is a good fellow, and will take an interest in the dear old place I was so fond of. You will be left as well off as I can manage. Don't worry yourself too much about me, but believe that I really do forgive you. Good-bye, good-bye.

"ANTHONY."

This letter, after he had directed and sealed it, was put carefully into a tin box on Mr. Gore's writing-table. It would not be posted until to-morrow. The other was a mere note—

" My dear Pettifer,

"It is some time since Ben had a lesson with his revolver. Will you and he, and your brother, who you said was coming to stay with you, come up and have a bit of lunch to-morrow at one, and we'll go to the range afterwards. I have good accounts of my wife, and Jos is going on as well as they could hope, but of course we are still very anxious.

"Ever yours,

"A. Gore."

Young Benjamin Pettifer was delighted when his father showed him the above note. He was often greatly bored at the vicarage, and these little expeditions to the Hall, together with the superior quality of the luncheon there, made an agreeable change. Moreover, he was becoming a fair shot with a revolver, and sometimes indulged in wild hopes that before long he would be able to equal Mr. Gore's feat of breaking the neck of a glass bottle at twenty-five yards' distance.

Anthony Gore, looking rather tired about the eyes, but otherwise much the same as usual, came out with his usual cheerful greetings to meet the Pettifers.

" My brother, Mr. Noel Pettifer," said the Vicar, introducing a spruce gentleman with a sharp face and red whiskers. " He is glad to have a breath of country air, as he is usually very busy in London."

" You've a very large solicitor's practice, haven't you ? " asked Anthony.

" Well, we don't exactly let the grass grow under our feet," replied Mr. Noel Pettifer, in a quick, dry voice. " Nice place this of yours, Mr. Gore. A good many pheasants, I expect, in those coverts over there ? "

" Pretty well. We're best off for rabbits. Come in ; lunch is just ready. Well, Ben, hope you'll distinguish yourself to-day. I've got a new revolver I want you to try."

The four gentlemen seated themselves round the luncheon-table.

"We'll have a bottle of old port," said Anthony cheerfully. "Keep up the system in this damp weather, eh, Pettifer? Here, Ben, take a glass; it'll binge you up, and you'll shoot all the straighter for it."

"When do you expect Mrs. Gore back?"

Anthony drained a glass of port to the dregs.

"Well, it depends on Jos," he answered slowly. "The little chap 'll pull through, I hope;" and he added, "I miss him helping me to feed the birds."

"I believe you are a first-class shot, Mr. Gore?" said the solicitor, in his crisp voice. "I am looking forward to seeing something of your skill."

"I suppose Ben has been cracking me

up," laughed the Squire. "Will you help me with another bottle of port?"

Long afterwards, Mr. Pettifer, recalling in future years the incidents of this day, used to dwell on his host's extreme cheerfulness during luncheon.

"I never saw the poor dear fellow in better spirits," he would remark. "Full of chat, and everything looking so bright in the future for him. How inscrutable are the ways of Providence!"

"You'll all three have a cigarette and a cup o' coffee?" said Tony. "We'll start after that; I've a revolver belonging to a friend of mine, and Ben shall try my new one."

The letter to Renée was in the post-box now, and would reach her by the first post to-morrow morning.

Early that day Anthony had been seized with a desire to go and have a last look at the graves of his father and mother. But

on second thoughts he had repelled the
idea. Some passers-by might notice his
presence in the churchyard, and comment
afterwards on the fact. He was resolved to
do nothing out of his ordinary routine.

At about half-past two Mr. Gore and his
friends sauntered leisurely through the
woods towards the range. It was about
half a mile distant from the house, in a
copse of beech and fir. At the opposite
end from the iron figure of a man, which
was the target, stood a small wooden
summer-house with benches for lookers-on.
A rustic table and some chairs were outside
the doorway. Close by, two of Anthony's
workmen had just started felling a Spanish-
chestnut tree. They paused over their
work when they saw the four gentlemen
advancing towards the range. The air was
damp and oppressive, the woods full of
moisture, the pathways strewn with sodden
brown leaves. A thrush, in a tall beech

tree behind the summer-house, was beginning a disjointed song. A small sycamore
had been cut down not far from the doorway, and hundreds of rotten chips lay near
the round disk of the departed tree.

Anthony laid two revolvers on the rustic
table, and Ben placed a third alongside.

"Well, we may as well start now. Look
here, Ben, you shall begin with six shots at
fifteen yards. You ought to get five bull's-
eyes out of the six."

Young Pettifer fired rather wildly.

"Look out, that's a bad beginning," said
the Squire.

And the solicitor's lip curled with amuse-
ment.

"Try again, my boy, don't be nervous.
And fire quicker. That's better! Go on!
very good! There's a bull's-eye. Well
done—a second one!"

Then Mr. Gore took his revolver and
fired at twenty-five yards, a bull's-eye each

time. Afterwards with his left hand, while young Pettifer's eyes grew round with admiration, four bullets hitting the bull's-eye, and the other two within the next circle.

"You are really a remarkable shot, Mr. Gore," the solicitor remarked, a little patronizingly.

"Now, Ben, try again. Twenty yards this time, and change your revolver for this one."

Young Pettifer in his trepidation let off this new weapon too soon.

"For Heaven's sake be careful!" shouted the Squire. "You nearly potted me in the chest. And, Ben, remember, I told you, when your revolver's loaded, always hold the muzzle *down*. You've forgotten that again. Now go on!"

Benjamin, whether from excitement, or owing to the increased distance, shot badly.

"Never mind, here's another, loaded all ready. Try and do better this time."

His father and uncle and the two workmen, who had drawn nearer, watched Ben's efforts, which were still not very successful, with interest.

"You'll improve soon," said Tony encouragingly. "And I say, Ben, look here, mind what I tell you! You've left one cartridge in that first revolver. That's awfully careless of you." Here the Squire pressed the spring and the cartridge fell out on the grass. "That's the most dangerous thing in the world. Any one taking it up would think, perhaps, it wasn't loaded, and that plays the devil!"

Benjamin was profuse in his apologies, and once more, with perspiring forehead and set lips, took aim. All the lookers-on were standing with their backs to Mr. Gore. He took the unloaded revolver off the table, and put in two fresh cartridges, unseen by the spectators.

"Well done, Ben!" he cried, "that's the best round you've had. You're improving like steam! But don't forget what I told you about being careful. I had a warning once, when I was at college, with the fate of a poor chap who was playing the fool. Now what did he do,"—Anthony laid his hand on the revolver with which young Pettifer had first shot,—" but take it into his stupid head, *without looking*, that a revolver was not loaded, like this one of yours, Ben, *now*, thanks to my having taken your remaining cartridge out, as you saw. Well, they were all sky-larking about the place, and the poor chap takes it up,"— Mr. Gore, whose face had not grown a shade paler, here did the same,—" and then, for a stupid joke, to startle the other fellows, he holds it up to his mouth like this—just, you know, for a—"

There was a sharp crack, a loud report that echoed through the steaming damp woods. Anthony Gore fell heavily forwards, his face sinking into the sodden leaves.

"God Almighty!" cried the solicitor, "it *was* loaded, after all!"

He ran towards the prostrate figure, and his brother gave a loud cry. Young Benjamin was too paralyzed by fear and astonishment to utter a sound. In less than a second the two workmen had also joined the group. With reverent hands, one of them, assisted by the Vicar, had turned the body over. Tears ran down Mr. Pettifer's cheeks when he looked despairingly at the face of his old friend. It was very much blanched, and the eyes were open, glazed and staring into space.

Mr. Noel Pettifer had knelt down by the body. He had studied medicine at Guy's Hospital before finally adopting the law as a profession, and now enunciated his opinions in his crisp and unmelodious voice.

"The ball has lodged in the cerebellum, and death has been quite instantaneous!"

He laid his finger on Anthony Gore's motionless head.

"There is a slight effusion of watery blood," he continued, "do you see? Cerebro-spinal fluid. Poor fellow, what a ghastly thing! It is the most awful and extraordinary accident!"

The Vicar did not answer. He was still looking with bewildered and tearful eyes at the face of the man who had been such a kindly friend to him, the good landlord, the cheery companion, the Squire who had done so much to cheer the monotony of the lives of his poorer neighbours. It seemed incredible that he would never wring Anthony's hand again, never hear him speak.

"It is too terrible for his poor wife!" said the clergyman, when he spoke at last. "And she is already in sore trouble! Who will break the news to her? Oh, what inexplicable trials God sends us! His was

such a useful life, such an example to us all.
And so recently married too, with apparently
long happy years to come for him and Mrs.
Gore!"

And poor blundering Anthony, who
assuredly would not have contradicted a
word of all this had he been yet alive, lay
rigid on the trampled grass. His face was
now of a peculiar leaden gray, livid in hue,
but with no distortion of feature. Only the
lips looked blue and swollen. The clergyman knelt down again beside the body.

"God bless you, Anthony," he said in a
low voice. Was not that short prayer for
the erring dead heard, and granted?

Then gently and tenderly they lifted the
tall figure and bore it through the woods
towards the home of which Anthony had
been so fond. As they passed the beech
tree the thrush began to sing again, loudly
and sweetly, and a few shafts of sunlight
crept under the damp boughs and fell upon

the immovable features. It seemed then
as if a half-smile lighted up Anthony Gore's
kind square face. They bore him across a
plot of grass, into the main road, up to the
portico of his house. By that time the
bearers breathed heavily, and wiped the
perspiration off their foreheads. One or
two servants came running out, and there
were loud screams from the women.

"Hush!" said Mr. Pettifer. "Try to
be calm and quiet. It isn't so hard for you,
though I know you all loved him as a kind
master, as it is for his young wife. My
heart bleeds for her. I ask your prayers,
my friends, for her in her sorrow."

They laid him in a narrow bed, and
drew the window-curtains close. Then Mr.
Pettifer lighted two high candles, and
placed them at his head. Ben, now crying
bitterly, went to fetch some flowers, and
they strewed them on the dead man's breast.
The Vicar knelt down, and prayed long and

earnestly; and when the evening drew in, he walked as noiselessly as he could out of the silent room, turning his head to take one last look at his friend.

Blundering and foolish, perhaps, poor Anthony Gore had always been, but at least he was loyal to the last.

# CHAPTER XV.

MR. PETTIFER was sitting in his study, writing poor Anthony's funeral sermon, which was to be preached on the Sunday after his body should have been laid to rest. It was two days since the tragedy had occurred, and the Vicar was feeling very sad at heart. He had just put what he could not help thinking was rather an eloquent sentence on paper, when the door opened to admit Mrs. Pettifer, looking, as usual, rather forlorn and draggled.

"I am sorry to disturb you, my love, but I have been so worried by the way Noel talks."

"What do you mean?"

"He says," continued Mrs. Pettifer, shaking out a woollen antimacassar as she spoke, "that he has been thinking—well— I hardly know how to put it—that dear Mr. Gore's death—"

"*Well?*" cried Mr. Pettifer, sharply.

"Wasn't—perhaps, an accident!"

The Vicar rose to his feet, positively trembling with anger.

"Where is Noel?"

"He has gone into the garden to smoke. I *knew* you'd be very much put out."

The clergyman, leaving his MS. in disorder, seized his soft hat, and strode into the garden. The weather was very mild for the time of year, and the birds were twittering among the young purple buds on the trees. The solicitor was reposing on a tumble-down garden-seat, his legs stretched out on a chair, and he was smoking a large meerschaum pipe, in the shape of a female figure.

" What the—I mean what on earth have you been saying to my wife, Noel, about poor dear Anthony ? "

The solicitor opened his eyes very wide, and began stroking his red whiskers.

" Well, thinking over the incidents of this sad tragedy, it occurred to me that it may not have been such a pure accident as we, in the innocence of our hearts, imagined. That's all."

" It is a wicked suggestion ! "

" My dear fellow, don't fire up like that ! Poor Mr. Gore may have had some lamentable secret in his life that even *you* weren't aware of. It is rather unlikely that a sensible man, accustomed to the use of fire-arms—"

" Noel ! if you weren't my brother !—"

" Well, I won't breathe a word, of course, to any human being. It is no earthly concern of mine."

" It's just like you lawyers," said the

Vicar, trembling, " you always want to make
a 'case' out of everything. You forget,
with all your boasted knowledge, that truth
is often stranger a good deal than fiction.
I always say that, given a subject, you can
tell exactly what a woman or a lawyer will
say about it. They invariably jump to
foolish conclusions. You know nothing
about Mr. Gore. He was an excellent,
God-fearing man. He was happily married
to a beautiful young wife, who made his
home delightful. Without being very rich,
I'm sure he'd no financial worries. He
always paid ready money. He was in perfectly sound health, and, you yourself saw,
in excellent spirits ! "

The solicitor shrugged his shoulders.
" Well," he answered, " I give you my word
of honour not to breathe my suspicions to
any other living soul."

And Mr. Pettifer, still a good deal
agitated, went back to his sermon.

Anthony Gore's funeral took place in a
drenching storm of rain, which never ceased
to pour down during the whole service. It
was not unlike the weather of the day on
which not so very long ago he had brought
his bride home. Mr. Pettifer, in answer to
a letter of condolence to Renée, had received from her a short note, saying that
she feared that she would not be able to
stand the strain of the service. But there
were many friends of Tony's gathered
around his grave. There was Frank Hesseltine, looking rather old and very sad, Lord
Wheldale, and Admiral Mullins, and country
neighbours, all deeply shocked at the tragic
end of the young Squire, from far and near.
There were well-to-do farmers, stolid labouring men, and weeping servants; a deputa-
tion of Oddfellows and another of Free
Foresters, and part of a troop of yeomanry;
the Mayor and some of the corporation
from the county town; and the member

for Anthony's division of the county. Mr.
and Lady Mary Prosser had sent a wreath
of colossal proportions; and the nine
Pettifer children had clubbed their pocket-
money together to buy another.

On the Sunday following the funeral the
little church was filled to overflowing. Mr.
Pettifer's voice grew hoarse and uncertain
more than once, and most of his simple-
minded hearers were moved to tears of
genuine sorrow during his discourse. The
Vicar touched on the joyful home-coming of
the late Squire and his young wife such a
short time ago; on their presence at the last
cheerful village gathering; on Anthony's
unflagging interest in the welfare of his less
prosperous friends; on his cheery greeting
whenever he met them, the kindly voice
that was now hushed for ever into silence.
But it was when Mr. Pettifer, in tones of
yet deeper emotion, alluded to the loneliness
and despair of the widow whom Mr. Gore

had left to mourn his loss, that the audience were most moved. Poor old "Aunt Isabella" had to be guided out of church by an attendant scarcely less tottery than herself. Mrs. Pettifer, in the front pew, fairly burst into tears. Mr. Noel Pettifer alternately caressed his red whiskers and studied his hymn-book. He did not look at his brother during the preaching of the latter's sermon, for fear of meeting his eye.

Frank Hesseltine returned to Ledsham Towers on the day after he had attended the funeral of his old friend. He had written a kind and sympathetic letter to Renée, for although he never for one moment imagined her to be in love with her husband, he considered her an excellent wife, and was afraid that the horror of the shock might injure her health.

Léontine's life at her Yorkshire home had not been very bright of late. There was still the same reserve, often drifting into coldness, in her husband's manner towards her, although he honestly tried to treat her with gentleness and consideration.

Once or twice Frank wondered what his wife had thought when she found that she had left her letter to Lord Huddersfield behind her. No doubt when she had met her old lover at the theatre they must have talked about it. Did she fancy that she had dropped it out of doors, or that it was eventually posted, and somehow or other never reached its destination? Hesseltine would never know. Once, when Frank caught Léontine's pleading glance resting upon him, he wondered whether she had guessed the truth, that it was he himself who had found and read what she had written? But there was surely nothing to be gained by an explanation; he must be content—and he smiled bitterly to himself— with " a measure of affection, and her entire esteem!"

Had Hesseltine been less sensitive and humble as to his own powers of winning and keeping a woman's love, or had there been less than twenty years' difference in age between the two, perhaps they might yet have arrived at an understanding. Every day, on the contrary, the breach between the two appeared to widen. Frank attributed a good deal of his wife's increasing depression to the news of Lord Huddersfield's projected marriage ; Léo's heart ached despairingly over the belief that Renée Gore had stolen her husband's affection from her. So the days went on.

The Thorowgoods drove over to tea, and were astonished to see how ill Mrs. Hesseltine looked.

"What the dickens is up with her?" said Mr. Thorowgood to his wife. "She's lost all her spirits. Ah! I expect she's been fagging herself to death in that filthy London!"

Miss Thorowgood, who at one time had indulged in wild dreams that she might herself have become the lady of Ledsham Towers, was always a little jealous of Léontine.

"She's losing her looks dreadfully, papa! With that flaxen hair you want colour in the cheeks. And she has such dark rings round her eyes!"

"They're the most beautiful eyes *I* ever saw!" said Léo's faithful admirer, old Squire Thorowgood. "And Mrs. Hesseltine's a woman who'll be good-looking to the end of her days. There's breeding for you! None of your hairy-heeled ones there!"

Mr. Wordie, who was also at Ledsham Towers, had not failed to notice the change in his adored Mrs. Hesseltine. Léo was very much touched at his pathetic little efforts to entertain her. He read aloud to her rather dull little stories, of his own choosing, on week-days, and hymns on Sundays. During the day, when he was not busy in the library, he trotted about paying visits to the in- and out-door servants, and taking the deepest interest in all their concerns. But his gossiping was always of a perfectly harmless quality.

A few days after Frank's return, he mentioned to his wife one morning at breakfast that he had heard from Mrs. Gore.

"How is she?" asked Léo. "And dear little Jos? I can't bear to think of him so ill."

"She is evidently miserable about the child," said Frank, compassionately. "Poor thing! she *has* had a hard time of it. And Mr. Morant's state is, I fear, hopeless too. She says, Léo, in this letter, that she is anxious to have an interview with me in London as soon as possible. I thought, therefore, of going up to Carlton Gardens to-morrow morning."

Léontine's heart swelled. "May I come too?"

"Of course, dear, you can come and go whenever you choose."

"Then I'll start to-morrow. I am sorry Louise Valendar has gone back to Germany."

Mr. Hesseltine did not answer. He was reading Mrs. Gore's letter through again.

Mr. Wordie's owl-like white face appeared at the doorway.

"Should you," he asked, timidly, "have any objection to my taking dinner at the Farm to-day? Mr. and Mrs. Frost have kindly invited me."

"Not a bit," said Léo. "You must consider yourself at home here, Mr. Wordie. And I wanted to tell you we have to go to London to-morrow, but we hope—don't we, Frank?—that you'll stay on here just the same."

"Of course, of course," assented Frank, absently. "And," he added, "I dare say,

Léo, you would ask Mrs. Gore—send a message, I mean, through me, when I write to-day—if she'd dine quite quietly alone with us in Carlton Gardens?"

"Certainly, as you wish it." Léo spoke in freezing tones.

"Well, if you don't feel sympathy with her, left alone, and wearing herself out with looking after a sick child, I can't help it."

Mr. Hesseltine pushed back his chair, rose, and left the room. His temper had certainly not improved of late. Even Mr. Wordie noticed his tone, and felt sorry for Léo, but it was impossible for him to say a word. He went slowly away.

\*   \*   \*   \*

Punctual to the time of his appointment, Frank Hesseltine sprang out of a hansom at the door of the flat in Victoria Street where Mrs. Gore was staying. He was shown into a rather dreary sitting-room, which bore but few traces of Renée's presence, as

there were no flowers, and scarcely a book
upon the tables. There was an india-rubber
plant in one window, some pampas grass
dyed rose-colour in a corner, and several
misty photographic groups hung on the
walls, which were covered with a hideous
paper, of brown scrolls on a slate-coloured
ground. The fire had evidently only been
recently lighted, the chintzes were faded,
the carpet was shabby. Frank stood at the
window, watching rows of carriages approaching the co-operative stores, and the
ladies hopping over the mud with their
petticoats gathered high above their boots.
The ubiquitous mechanical piano was at
work lower down the street,—it had been
sent further off owing to the presence of the
little sick boy in the house ; a starved-look-
ing woman was holding out bunches of
narcissus to passers-by, who usually snubbed
her.

The door behind Frank opened, and Mrs.

Gore entered. She was dressed in a clinging gown of black cashmere, her hair
knotted on her neck as usual, and no
widow's cap on her head, of which Frank
was glad, for he detested them. He took
both her hands in his and wrung them
warmly. He felt that this silent sympathy
was the best that he could offer.

Renée's face was for her very pale. All
her colour had concentrated itself into two
small patches on her cheek-bones. There
were black rings round her eyes, and the
lids were red and swollen.

She motioned him to a chair facing the
window, and sat down with her back to the
light. There was a long pause. Then
Frank spoke.

"It is needless to say how much I have
thought of you. Are you happier now
about the boy ? I earnestly hope so."

Her voice shook a little.

"No ; the doctor takes a despairing view.

His darling little face is so much altered.
I sometimes think I shall go mad when I
look at it!"

"You have indeed had an awful time of
it—one thing after another. I wish with
all my heart I could do anything to help or
comfort you."

"Yes, it has been hard. I am getting
worn out, but that is of no consequence.
No, I don't want pity. But to-day I also
had bad news of my dear father. I go up
and down between the two—for father is
in Surrey. I cannot stay there, because I
must see how the child is at night, and
early in the morning, when his temperature
falls." There was a sob in her voice as she
ended—"They give my father only a few
months to live. My dear old nurse is
failing too, and if . . . the boy goes, I
shall be left always alone."

Frank's own eyes grew misty.

"Dear Mrs. Gore, it is terrible for you!

But I still hope for Jos. Children have such wonderful rallying powers."

Mrs. Gore rose from her chair, and stood up on the hearthrug. Her face had grown almost ghastly.

"Do you know why I sent for you?" The sentence was spoken so low, that Hesseltine only just caught the words.

"I hope, because I am an old friend, and can feel for you with my whole heart!"

Frank had settled with himself that it would be best not to allude to the tragic circumstances of Anthony's death, unless Mrs. Gore herself should begin to speak on the subject. Moreover, in a previous letter he had told her how deeply he felt for her, and how true his regard had been for his faithful friend now gone from them.

She looked away from him.

"It was because, though I am not a religious woman, far from it, I am a curiously superstitious one."

" Yes ! "

" And I have a fancy—an absorbing idea it has grown to be now—that the illness of little Jos, who is so sweet and innocent, is intended as a punishment for me."

" That is surely morbid. You are over-strained, or you wouldn't imagine such a thing for a moment."

" It isn't fancy ; I deserve all the punishment I could have. Don't look sorry for me, you will not soon. We shall probably never meet again after to-day."

A notion flashed across Frank's mind that Mrs. Gore, from the effects of fatigue and sorrow, was now wandering and not responsible for her words. She went on, speaking more quickly—

" I have behaved infamously to you ! I should never have confessed it, perhaps,— I am not one to regret my actions as a rule,—had it not been for little Jos. I have thought that he might die if I did not tell you."

She was walking up and down the room now, looking white as a lily in her clinging black drapery. Frank fixed his eyes anxiously upon her.

" Remember," she said, stopping suddenly in front of him, "*I don't ask you to forgive me !* I don't *wish* you to do so. I care for nothing any longer, excepting that that little child should not suffer."

" Dear Mrs. Gore, what can you mean ? We have always been the best of friends ! "

" Ah ! Do you remember a letter from your wife to Lord Huddersfield ? "

Frank started up from his chair, and moved a step nearer to Mrs. Gore.

" What, in God's name, do you mean ? "

" You read it one morning at Crabston ! You have been drifting apart from your wife ever since. *I* wrote that letter ! "

Frank Hesseltine stared blankly at her.

Was he dreaming? All power of speech failed him.

"*I* wrote it, I repeat, because I wished to make your wife miserable. Ah! you see I don't mince matters! I had the best reason for hating her. But she has never done *you* wrong. I threw out hints about her before to you to make you anxious and suspicious, and succeeded. The letter was my trump card. I have said I don't want you to forgive me."

Frank Hesseltine clenched his hands.

"It was a—a vile thing to do! If you were a man, I should use a stronger word!"

"If I were a man you could knock me down, you could call me out and shoot me at Boulogne. I wish to Heaven I were!"

"What could have made you, *you*, the wife of my old friend, treat us like this?"

"Cannot you guess? What makes a woman revengeful? You may as well stay patiently and hear me out, Mr. Hesseltine.

I wished as a girl to marry Lord Huddersfield ; he had given me to understand—well, never mind all that, but he afterwards fell in love with Countess Léontine Wartburg. She was fond of him then ; but she fell still more in love with *you* after she married ! How dense you were not to find that out ! And she is in love with you now."

Frank Hesseltine's heart was beating so loudly he almost thought that Renée must have heard it. A flood of joy seemed to engulf him, to absorb all other feelings in its passionate current, even, for a few moments at least, the one of justifiable anger towards the woman confronting him. Something of his feelings was evident to her.

" May we not as well say good-bye now, Mr. Hesseltine ? I shall never ask you to take my hand again, but I have told you the truth, not out of remorse, not out of pity for your wife, but for the love of my little boy. I knew he could never get well till I had confessed my—I suppose sins you would call them, to you ! You can go back and be happy ever after with Léo. Forget me in my loneliness and despair as soon as you can."

" You wouldn't believe me," said Frank, in a low voice, " if I *did* say I forgave you, yet. Perhaps some day. . . . But you might have broken *her* heart for ever. It was the sort of infernal ingenuity of which no one but a woman could have been capable ! You tried to poison my mind long before your crowning piece of cruelty ! But I shall always think very tenderly of Jos. Not only for his own sake, but for what he has been the means of giving back to me."

She did not answer. Her face was turned away from him. The monotonous roll of wheels, the street music growing fainter, alone broke the stillness.

Frank Hesseltine turned silently away,

and went slowly out of the room. From a neighbouring door the face of a hospital-nurse in a white cap looked out. Frank stopped and went towards her.

"May I look at the child?" he asked.

"He's asleep," said the woman in a whisper, and walking on tip-toe she led him into a half-darkened room. There was a screen round the bed, and only a feeble light from a lamp lit up Jos's nursery. Frank bent tenderly over the small pinched face, with its cropped yellow hair—the face so strangely unlike that of his merry little Jos, with whom he had romped and laughed many times. He did not dare to kiss the damp forehead, for fear of awakening the child, but with tears standing in his eyes he moved gently away. The canary-bird was half asleep, the toys were put by, and in another room close at hand a broken-hearted woman was sitting alone, too despairing perhaps even to weep.

# CHAPTER XVI.

## " AND KISSED AGAIN WITH TEARS."

LÉONTINE was sitting in her little boudoir, a piece of silk embroidery lying on her knee. She was not a great worker at any time, but to-day it was simply impossible for her to keep her attention fixed on any book whatsoever. Her zither, which she had hardly touched for weeks, was on the table beside her, with a broken string. Owing to the situation of the house, but little noise from the outside world was borne in upon her, and it was too chilly as yet for the birds to begin to sing.

She was startled from a sad reverie by

Frank's entrance. She scarcely looked at
him as he came in, and merely made some
commonplace remark about the cold. He
came close up to her.

"Léo," he said, "I have been to see Mrs.
Gore."

What need was there to tell her that?
She winced a little as he spoke.

"Léo, my darling, my darling, look up at
me!"

She turned quickly towards him, puzzled
and trembling. It was the voice of her old
lover that was speaking again. Her lips
slightly parted, the large violet eyes fixed
upon him, she remained silent. He knelt
down by her low chair, and drew her
towards him.

"I have come, my Léo, my beloved, to
ask you to forgive me!"

"Oh, Frank, what is it? What do you
mean?"

His head was bowed before her. In the

bright light which fell from the window upon it, she noticed how old he seemed to have grown. The lines round his eyes were ever so much deeper than they had been a year ago. But worn and haggard as he seemed in this hour of humiliation, he was still the same man who had wooed and won her in the past, and the one whom she loved now as she had never loved him then. For all answer he drew the little flaxen head close to his breast, and kissed the soft curls.

"I have been so base, so cruel to you, little Léo. In all my life to come I can never undo it. I have failed to make you happy. I have gone very near to breaking your heart!"

Her tears fell upon his hands.

"What has happened, Frank? what has changed since—since this morning? You are not angry with me now, then? I thought you didn't care about me any more. It was very hard, but I have tried to be patient!"

"*Care* for you!" The passion in his voice made her form quiver. "I always loved you madly, but now I cannot frame any words in which to express what I feel for you. It wasn't *all* my fault though, Léo, my own darling. People told me lies about you. That you were tired of me! And I didn't wonder at it. Only it made me so miserable, I hardly knew sometimes what I said or did."

He kissed her again and again.

"Frank, can you tell me a little what it was that they said, those people who were unkind about me? And why it was? I didn't think I had done harm to anybody."

"Harm! *you*, my angel! But there is some wickedness so great you wouldn't understand it. I may just tell you a little. I fancied you liked Huddersfield still. Don't

look angry, little woman, because if you
*had*, it might have been excusable—"

"I was fond of him once, Frank ; I ought
to have told you, perhaps. But soon after
I married you I began to feel so differently
about you. It was a much greater, deeper
affection than I had ever known before. It
seemed to absorb me. And then, when I
thought we were going to be so happy,—forgive me, Frank darling,—I imagined that
some one else had made you like *her*
best !"

"You silly little child ! Do you know
that again and again when I have been
talking to her (I know whom you mean), I
have hungered for a sound of your voice ;
that I almost grew tired of her beauty,
when I thought of your dear little face !"

"I was so sure you were fond of her !"

"I liked her as a man likes a handsome
lively woman who is always charming to
him. Yes, I was fond of her, in a sense ;

and I thought her a good wife and a good woman."

Léo did not ask more questions. She was too well satisfied with her present happiness to care to know how it had been brought about. Her eyes were still swimming with tears, and her head was resting on her husband's shoulder. And he felt as if he could not loosen his arms ; she was so much more his own now than she had ever been before. He stroked the yellow curls with one hand.

"Are there any two people in the whole world, Léo, as happy now as you and I ?"

Many men and women have said the same, and thousands yet unborn will repeat the like foolish words, maybe, but never a pair will utter them with more truth and conviction.

"What a lucky husband and wife we are, Léo ! All the love-making to come over again, at a time when people usually begin to be prosaic!"

She smiled, and lifted her face to kiss him.

"It is too good to be real, Frank! Let us never think of these last months again."

And then they talked in the happy, foolish way in which lovers have conversed since the days of Eden. If Léo knew that there were things connected with the past that her husband did not wish to tell her, this was to her now a matter of complete indifference. When two friends meet again in the other world after a long parting, it is most likely of the joys of reunion that they speak—not of the pain, and illness, and death that once severed their lives.

When she went up-stairs to dress for dinner, her voice was carolling out one of her native German airs, loudly and sweetly, like a bird who knows that the spring is near at hand.

After a short stay at Ledsham Towers the Hesseltines returned to London, as the lilacs and mays were in bloom, and the laburnums a perfect shower of gold in the gardens opposite Léo's boudoir.

Laughing and talking, the two were strolling homewards through the park, when a little way off, crossing over from Stanhope Gate, they saw a bath-chair, and a tall figure in black walking beside it.

Léo stopped. "It is Mrs. Gore!" she said, with rather a rising colour.

"So it is! And poor little Jos! I heard he was better, dear little man. Hadn't we better go over to the other side, though, Léo, so as to avoid them? I don't particularly wish to meet Mrs. Gore."

"Frank . . . . . would you mind sitting down and waiting for me? I should *like* to go and speak to them."

He looked down with a kind smile into his wife's deep violet eyes.

"As you wish, darling!"

"Well then, sit upon this bench, and I will walk on as quickly as I can, and catch them up."

Léontine hurried down the broad gravelled path, and panting a little with her exertions, overtook the bath-chair being drawn across the park in the direction of Albert Gate.

"Mrs. Gore!" she said, in a trembling voice.

The lady in black turned her head sharply round. She was more beautiful perhaps than ever, in the severe simplicity of her dress, although her face was thinner and paler, and seemed to be that of an older woman than when Léo had last seen her. Renée's lips were set in expression that was not altogether pleasant. She was terribly afraid of what she would have called a "scene," especially in the presence of the child. She could not imagine why her former rival should have sought her out,

unless it were to proffer her a formal forgiveness, which she felt would be altogether
unendurable.   Léo's calm manner, however,
quickly reassured her.

Mrs. Hesseltine held out her hand and
merely said, as if they had met a few days ago,

" I was so anxious to see dear little Jos !
It is delightful that he is well enough to be
out again !"

She bent down and kissed the child.
Renée's eyes softened.

" Yes, he is better, but still very weak."

She looked down with infinite tenderness
at the boy.   His small face was drawn and
pinched, and his golden curls shorn away.
He had the peculiarly listless air of a child
who has been dangerously ill, and is still
very feeble.

Léo held his little gloved hand in hers.

" You must tell me, darling, what toy
you would like me to send you.   Anything
in the whole world that you can fancy."

Jos was leaning languidly back in his chair. He looked up at his Aunt Renée.

" Think of something, my sweet. It is very kind of Mrs. Hesseltine, isn't it ? "

" It's Léo," said the little fellow, laying his fingers on those of his old friend. " Léo, I should like a rocking-horse, with real harness, and a skin coat ! "

Renée's lip quivered. She was thinking how long it would be perhaps before the weak little frame would be able to make use of the toy.

" Certainly, darling. And Frank will send you something too."

For the first time that day Jos smiled a wan little smile.

" I should like a whole regiment of cavalry."

" All right, you shall have them, great big soldiers."

Léo kissed him again. He had several old toys with him in his bath-chair, including

a sailor doll with a broken nose. Mrs.
Hesseltine admired them all, and asked
questions about the sailor, which ended by
Jos's adding that he thought he would like
to have a large ship too.

"Good-bye, Renée," said Léontine at
last. "I am sure he will become stronger
every day now the spring has come. I will
send him some flowers when I get home."

Then these two women, whose paths had
crossed each other so strangely, shook hands
in a perfectly calm and friendly manner, by
the side of the bath-chair, and Léo went
back to join her husband, turning more than
once to kiss her hand to the sick child.

Mr. and Mrs. Hesseltine were both a little
silent as they retraced their steps. Walking
down Piccadilly, they noticed a large awning
over one of the doors, through which came
a vision of palm trees, and bushes of coloured
blooms. A few loafers were gathered about
the portico, and on the red carpet were frag-

ments of white satin ribbon, grains of rice, and stray flowers, fallen doubtless from bouquets.

" Ah," said Frank, " that's old MacGwire Jones's house. Of course—the wedding was to-day ! I suppose Lady Huddersfield was a mass of diamonds."

" I'm sure I hope it'll turn out happily," said Léo, cheerfully. " There would be a great deal of good in Lord Huddersfield if he were married to a sensible woman. They say she's clever, and will keep him in order."

" I dare say. I'm not at all cynical, Léo. I quite believe in the influence of a charming sensible girl, with experience and tact. Hallo ! there's Prosser riding ! How fat he's grown ; but he's got a good weight-carrying cob !"

And Mr. Prosser here takes off his very polished hat with a gracious smile, and looking more smug and prosperous than ever, ambles away out of Piccadilly, and these pages as well.

When June came, and the roses were in bloom again over all the land, the Hesseltines left London to spend ten days in the villa by the Rhine once more. It might have been only yesterday that they had seen it last, with its sweet dreamy garden, and quiet sunny rooms.

And, his arm thrown around his wife's slender shoulders, Frank walks with her under the trellised vines on the evening of their arrival ;

"The musk from the rose is blown"

into their faces, the river flowing through shadow and moonbeams at their feet.

Once more he told her of his love, deeper and of stronger fibre now ; and the fervour of her eyes took the place of responsive words.

When they came back at last into the sitting-room, the pair stood silent for a moment before the portrait of the little dead Countess.

And Frank Hesseltine hesitated.

Should he tell Léontine now the story of her mother, and of another tie which bound him still more closely to them both? The moonlight shone on the pictured face, and on his wife's flaxen curls. The bats flitted past the window, balmy gusts of air floated in, rustling the curtains of old green brocade, and bringing with them the perfume of many flowers.

Then he felt that it would be worse than an error, a sin perhaps, to disturb all this calm and sweetness by any tragic memory. It were wiser and better, surely, to let the secret of that pathetic face looking down on them be laid asleep for ever.

If the dead lovers whose hearts had been so cruelly wrung many a year agone in this same quiet room could have looked down upon these other two—the friend of one, the child of both,—with arms entwined, and happy eyes and lips that met, they might perhaps have seen in them a symbol of forgiveness and peace, of the mercy held out at last to all who have suffered, and wept, and sinned.

And here we may leave Frank Hesseltine and his wife awhile, with no lurking fears of what time may bring to them. Should the duration of their lives be brief, they will yet have known more joy than is often scattered through long months and years; should they, on the contrary, go hand in hand through many moons of shine and shadow, we need not be afraid. For then theirs will surely only be

> " A life that overlong may prove,
>   For passion or for power,
>   But too too short for that still love
>   Which blesses every hour."

THE END.

www.ingramcontent.com/pod-product-compliance
Lightning Source LLC
Chambersburg PA
CBHW021054030726
47496CB00006B/1832